how t

i Love

you

Sw♥♥n
Reads
Swoon Reads   New York

A SWOON READS BOOK
An Imprint of Feiwel and Friends

Swoon Reads books may be purchased for business or promotional use.
For information on bulk purchases, please contact the Macmillan
Corporate and Premium Sales Department at (800) 221-7945 x5442
or by e-mail at specialmarkets@macmillan.com.

Library of Congress Cataloging-in-Publication Data

Cozzo, Karole.
How to say I love you out loud / Karole Cozzo. — First edition.
pages cm
Summary: When Jordyn's autistic brother joins her at her elite school
her junior year, she is determined not to let anyone know they are
related, even if that means closing herself off to her closest friends
Erin, Tanu, and Alex, the football captain she secretly loves.
ISBN 978-1-250-06359-5 (paperback) — ISBN 978-1-250-06362-5 (e-book)
[1. High schools—Fiction. 2. Schools—Fiction. 3. Brothers and
sisters—Fiction. 4. Autism—Fiction. 5. Dating (Social customs)—
Fiction. 6. Family life—Fiction.] I. Title.
PZ7.1.C695How 2015
[Fic]—dc23
2014049322

Book design by Anna Booth

Feiwel and Friends logo designed by Filomena Tuosto

First Edition: 2015

10 9 8 7 6 5 4 3 2 1

macteenbooks.com

To my Luxie Lou and Christian J—
never, ever give up on your dreams

& Mr. H, for never letting me give up on mine

Author's Note

I've had the privilege of serving children with disabilities and their families in the public and private school settings for the past decade. I have the utmost appreciation and respect for their bravery, strength, perseverance, and resilience as they confront challenges big and small. My experiences with these families did, in part, inspire some of the content of this book and prompt the messages about acceptance and advocacy included within. However, this story is a work of fiction and any resemblance to actual persons or events is purely coincidental.

Chapter One

There's a particular kind of energy radiating from school on the first day, part nervous freshman energy, part rambunctious senior energy, and part look-how-I-reinvented-myself-over-the-summer energy. The vibe is the same every year, at any given school, even as the students change, as the timid freshmen become bored sophomores and a new graduating class takes over. The excitement will, very predictably, dissipate by Friday, but on the Tuesday after Labor Day, the return of students turns the school and parking lot into a veritable beehive alive with the buzz of frantic activity and socializing.

As I walk toward the front door, Erin Blackwell struggles to catch up with me while holding her Dunkin' Donuts coffee cup steady, her designer flip-flops slapping the concrete. "Hi, Jordyn," she greets me tersely.

"Hey, Erin. What's wrong?"

It's only 7:42 a.m., and we haven't even stepped into the building yet. I don't know how or why she already looks stressed, but she does. Erin is sort of perpetually stressed. As are a lot of kids at Valley Forge High School.

As am I a lot of the time, if I'm being honest. Stress is absorbed through osmosis around here.

"Ugh." Erin shakes her head in disgust. "It took me forever to get my contacts in, so my hair started to frizz, and it's so humid that the waves wouldn't hold when I finally did get around to doing it. The drive-through at Dunkin' was backed up, like, a mile, and they forgot to put the caramel in my cappuccino anyway. Which is all really unfortunate because now I'm late, and I look a hot mess, and I have A.P. Bio first period. I think Bryce is in my section, and it would have been really nice to actually feel like I have my shit together before walking in there." Finally she remembers to breathe. "How can I be so far behind before the day's even started?"

Erin's anxiety is so potent, I need to take a deep breath of my own.

Erin is a doe-eyed Bella Thorne look-alike, and I assess her long, strawberry-blond locks. "Your hair looks gorgeous. You look gorgeous. We still have twelve minutes before the homeroom bell. And I thought things were getting better with Bryce?"

She'd had a rough summer as she tried to move on from their dramatic breakup in June.

"They are. It's just hard being back at school." She frowns. "Makes me feel like things should go back to the way they were last year. Plus, I don't really feel like hearing him join in on all that BS where the guys rate the hottest freshman girls, ya know?"

"Well, I think you're one of the hottest junior girls." I smile and tug on the bottom of one impeccably curled strand of her hair. "He's going to see you and regret everything."

"Everything" being the girl from the Shipley School he hooked up with behind Erin's back.

Erin stops in her tracks and looks at me, chewing her lip. "Really? You think he'll even notice?"

I take a final deep breath as we approach the front door. It's only 7:43 and already I'm exhausted. "Positive."

We push into the fray and are swept up in the tide of students moving through the lobby. Dana Travers, senior cocaptain of the varsity field hockey team, rushes past us, sending a reminder over her shoulder. "Practice starts *on time* today, ladies. No first day excuses."

I nod, even though I lack Dana's zeal for competitive team sports. But I need some kind of athletic activity to round out my college applications and I'm a decent midfielder, so hockey it is.

A group of students from the exclusive Musicians' Guild are already disassembling their instruments after what must have been a very early morning rehearsal. As we move through the shifting crowd, which emits loud voices and sweaty energy, I notice a serious-looking kid leaning against the wall and pushing his glasses up his nose as he reads a physics textbook, one overachiever of many. We haven't even been to *homeroom* yet.

The atmosphere in the lobby leaves me feeling dazed and sluggish, and I struggle to wrap my head around the frenzy. I'm still on summer time. Life was much more relaxed when I was peddling Philly soft pretzels at the tennis club poolside snack bar, chatting with Alex when he appeared at the side window covered in dirt and grass clippings during a break from the hot sun and the demands of keeping the golf course pristine with the rest of the grounds crew.

To be honest, though, there's a part of me that has a hard time keeping pace with the student body at Valley Forge regardless of the season. This will be my second year at Valley Forge High School. My family moved to Berwyn from Lansdale, a town about thirty minutes away, last summer. At my old school, most kids didn't really care that much about their grades or extracurricular activities, knowing they'd end up in nearby state schools. My new classmates always seem to be looking over their shoulders to see who might be gaining on them. Last year, I felt like at the same time people were sizing me up as a new friend, they were assessing me as some kind of potential threat. To their class rank. To their first-chair position in orchestra. To their acceptance letter from Princeton.

I don't get it, or maybe they just don't get *me*. I prefer to fly under the radar, and I'm sure as hell not trying to steal anyone's spotlight. I hate the feeling of eyes on me, always have. I've had way too many eyes on me over the years, even if they weren't on *me*, per se. Even after a year, I'm still not sure how well I fit in here. Crammed like a sardine in the small upper lobby waiting for the homeroom bell, I feel strangely alone and disconnected.

Then I catch sight of something familiar, propped against the foot of one of the old wooden benches. It's a worn black JanSport, with ALEX written in Wite-Out across the front pocket. I perk up at once, instantly feeling more grounded. Alex is around here somewhere. He'll throw me my favorite smile—the one that makes it seem like we're laughing at some joke no one else gets—and this place won't seem as serious or intense.

Suddenly, I can't wait to see him. We haven't talked much in the past few weeks, because his family was on vacation and he stopped working at the club when two-a-days started for the football team. Sometimes I'd see him down by the field after our evening practices, but most nights he seemed kind of distracted, überfocused on football, I guess. Alex isn't the best player in the world. No matter how many wind sprints he runs or how much time he spends in the weight room, he's perpetually second string. You can tell it annoys the crap out of him, this one thing Mr. Perfect can't be perfect at. I find his frustration sort of endearing. And the rest of the team must find his persistence admirable, because they elected him cocaptain, second-string skills and all. He's just got those natural leadership genes, like a young, half Hispanic Barack Obama or something.

Alex is good people. And as if to prove my point, he walks through the door closest to the teacher lot, barely visible behind the tall stack of books he's carrying for Mrs. Higgins, our ancient librarian, who hobbles alongside him, smiling up in admiration.

I bite my lip to keep from giggling. My friend is such a Boy Scout. Seriously. I'm not kidding—he's an *actual* Boy Scout who's been working on this big Eagle Scout project in whatever spare time he has, which isn't much. But on a daily basis, he seems to go around earning merit badges in Helpfulness and Nobleness and all that good stuff.

"I'll be right back," I tell Erin, and take off in his direction.

He notices me over the top of the books and grins instantaneously. "Air Jordan, there you are!"

I smile in response to today's selection from his litany of ridiculous nicknames: Air Jordan . . . M.J. . . . Twenty-three . . . or as he called me for a while in Spanish class last year, Veintitrés.

I can't think of a single thing I have in common with the basketball icon Michael Jordan, other than my name, which is Jordyn Michaelson. I'm five foot three, with hazel eyes and wavy dark shoulder-length hair cut in layers. Female. And white—sadly so, being that summer just ended. But for whatever reason, Alex is amused by the stupid nicknames. Thing is, as stupid as I find them, it's impossible to look at his face when he's busy cracking himself up and not feel amused, too.

His brown eyes get all sparkly, and his wide grin of even white teeth gets all goofy. Combined with the close-cropped black hair and slight widow's peak, all I see is a little boy looking for mischief. Alex is one of those people who looks right *at* you, for real, and practically dares you to make mischief with him.

Hurrying toward him, I realize I'm opening my arms to give him a hug, even though hugging isn't something we usually do. There are unspoken boundaries we have not dared to cross, not even dared to *approach*, since last year. I'm so focused on Alex that I don't even notice Leighton Lyons, our other hockey co-captain, trotting across the lobby from the opposite direction, until we have a full-on collision. Our shoulders slam into each other's and I stumble backward, off balance, my heavy backpack nearly pulling me down.

I right myself and rub my shoulder, grumbling inwardly. Girl really needs to learn that other people inhabit this planet. Where is she headed in such a hurry?

When I look up, I get my answer, even though it's not one that makes sense. Not. At. All. I see her arms wrapped around Alex's torso, beating me to the punch with a hug. Then I watch as she does one better and plants a quick, flirty kiss upon his lips. "Hey, babe."

I stand and stare in disbelief, like an idiot, waiting for it to compute. Which it doesn't. Leighton hugging Alex. Leighton *kissing* Alex. Leighton calling Alex *babe*. What? When? How?

But none of it cuts as deeply as him casually looping his arm around her waist and turning to talk to me like none of this requires an explanation. Like none of this should bother me in any way. At least he has the decency to ask if I'm okay, which Leighton does not. "You alright, Jordyn?"

"Yeah, I'm fine."

Even though suddenly I'm not. There's a sick feeling in my gut as the realization sinks in that suddenly everything is different.

"Please," Leighton interjects. "She takes harder hits than that on the field every day." Pinching Alex's side, she smirks at him. I notice how they stand exactly eye to eye, the same height, and I feel small and insignificant. "We're just as tough as you guys, right, Jordyn?"

"Umm, sure."

"It's so good to see you," he says, smiling all the while, but rubbing her hand with the pad of his thumb while he says it. "I was so pissed I had to miss the staff party. You'll have to give me the recap."

I swallow my feelings and try not to bat an eye. "Yeah, it was quite the event. They added karaoke this year. And to be honest, I really would have been okay with summer ending without having to see Mr. Jacoby perform 'Happy' in a bathing suit."

Alex throws his head back and laughs, his full belly laugh, the one that always makes me feel like tiny seeds in my heart are blooming. His laughter nurtures some kind of longing that has no business being rooted there. His arm around Leighton's waist makes those little sprouts of wistfulness wilt and topple as quickly as they sprang up.

"Please tell me you were a backup dancer for him at least."

"Absolutely." I smile in spite of myself, in spite of the Leighton-shaped elephant in the room, and shake my head. "You know me so well."

"Did Petersen show up really drunk again?" he asks, referring to the president of the club. "Hit on any of the lifeguards who aren't even legal yet?"

Leighton tugs on the bottom of Alex's shirt before I get a chance to answer. "Hey, listen, I need to talk to you about some Athletic Council stuff real quick and I've got to run to the ladies' before homeroom, so can we . . ." She's talking to Alex but looking at me, waiting for me to make myself scarce.

"Yeah, sure, babe." He nods quickly, the word sounding even more wrong coming from his lips than hers. Alex tightens his grip on her and turns in the direction of the side hallway, where there's some space. He talks over his shoulder as they walk. "We'll catch up in history, okay, Michaelson?"

I nod, ignoring the tightness in my throat. Before, his use of my last name used to feel intimate. Now it reminds me that I'm a buddy and nothing more.

This is what you wanted, I remind myself as I turn away from the train wreck and walk back toward Erin, who's talking with our friend Tanu. *Just friends, right? You're lucky you walked away with that much.*

But I guess I'd thought . . . I guess I'd thought that somehow, by keeping him as a close friend, I could still call Alex mine. It was easy enough last year when he wasn't dating anyone. Having Alex as a best friend was an acceptable consolation prize when I couldn't have anything more. I'd grown comfortable with the idea and never given much thought to how things might change.

I sneak a quick peek over my shoulder. Leighton's back is against the wall and Alex has one arm above her head, keeping her in place, his body pressed against hers. I wonder what Athletic Council business has anything to do with their mouths mashed together like that.

Erin is much less discreet. She gapes, openmouthed, at the happy couple. "Wow, Leighton and Alex, really? When did that happen?"

"Oh, sometime this summer. Someone posted a picture on Facebook," Tanu says.

I wonder how many hours each day Tanu spends on Facebook. I also wonder if I'm the last person to know *everything*.

"It was this superhot picture," she continues, causing the sick feeling in my gut to flare up. "He's in his football jersey and she's all blond and tan. They're like . . . Tyler and Caroline from

Vampire Diaries, that's what it makes me think of. Or more specifically, you know when Tyler and Caroline kissed for the first time? Season two, episode twelve?"

"No, I don't know." Erin laughs. "We don't all have a photographic memory like you do."

"Anyway, that's what the picture looks like. They look so good together. And I want a boyfriend."

Now Erin is frowning again. "Me too. The two of them are just so perfect. That really makes me miss Bryce."

I square my shoulders and bite back my irritation. "Let's talk about something else." If campus is a beehive, Leighton is definitely its queen. And maybe I secretly call Alex Mr. Perfect. Somehow it doesn't translate into them being perfect *together*. At least not to me.

I engage them in other mindless gossip, trying to keep my thoughts away from the truth of the matter, which is that the sight of Alex and Leighton kissing really makes me miss someone, too.

But how can you miss someone you never really had?

What right do you have to miss someone when you were the person who walked away from them?

We continue on toward our respective homerooms.

I became friends with Erin and Tanu last fall, when we were all in the same English class together, and they're my best friends here at Valley Forge High School. But I'm not the kind of girl who shares every little detail about herself, even with my closest friends. School and home are two separate parts of my life, and as long as it stays like that . . . I don't know how "close" my girlfriends will ever really feel.

"Considering how humid it is today, does one of you have time to drop me off before practice? I really don't feel like walking."

Hockey practice is a bit of a sore subject with Tanu. She was also looking for a sport to complement the impressive academic and artistic sections of her résumé, but she didn't make the cut after tryouts in July.

Erin shakes her head, strawberry-blond curls flying. "Oh, hell no. You know I would if I could, but I'm not going to be the person walking onto the field late. Leighton would have my ass. She thinks it's really important for us to be on time."

Most things that are important to Leighton are important to Erin. Leighton is sort of her role model. Maybe even her idol.

"It's, like, a six-minute round trip!"

"Still. I don't feel like chancing it. Leighton says . . ."

I clamp my lips together to keep from groaning. Erin, God love her, starts way too many sentences with "Leighton says."

". . . everyone always takes the guys' sports teams so much more seriously than the girls'. If we want to be taken seriously, and given as much credit for our hard work, we have to take *ourselves* seriously."

I consider offering Tanu a ride myself, but truthfully, I don't want to end up in Leighton's line of fire, either. Even if I find her intensity a little dramatic and largely unnecessary.

I wave good-bye to my friends as the bell rings. I'm alone again, and without the stream of chitchat to distract me, the scary feeling returns—like I'm slipping out to sea, as the one person I counted on to keep me anchored around here is now tied to someone else.

My morning passes in a quick blur. Homeroom. A.P. Psychology and Sociology. English Literature. I'm anxious to get to Advanced Placement U.S. History, even though the size of my textbook rivals that of a med school anatomy reference book and the essay tests are rumored to be a bitch. At least I'll get to talk to Alex. Alone. He'll give me some kind of explanation for that scene in the lobby. He has to, right?

I pick a desk in the front left corner, pull out a fresh notebook, and wait. Just before the bell rings, Alex ambles in, book bag hanging loosely from his shoulders. I perk up without meaning to; at the sight of him my heart drops into my stomach, where it flutters around like a happy butterfly.

He's not yours, I berate my poor, delusional organ. *Silly for you to act like that.*

But it's hard not to react, and my chest constricts with something like pain as I study him. The best part of his arrival has nothing to do with how good he looks, or how good he smells, for that matter. It's the *way* he looks, which is right at me, like no one else is in the room. His eyes brighten and crinkle at the edges, his easy grin blooms, and he makes a beeline for the empty seat behind me.

"M.J., thank goodness." He slides into the seat and taps the back of my chair with his foot. "What's happening? How's your day been since I saw you last?"

"It's been good. Same ol', same ol'."

"Missed you in Spanish. It was boring without you."

"I don't feel bad for you. I don't know why you don't just test out."

Alex's full name is Alejandro and when he forgets to downplay it, his accent is spot-on. Last year he entertained himself by capturing our teacher and classmates in perfect caricature on my paper textbook cover.

"It's alright. I like having *one* class where I can actually coast." His brow wrinkles in confusion as he stares at my notebook. "Didn't you get your iPad?"

"Oh, right." I shake my head, because I don't think it was really necessary for every student in the building to be issued a brand-new iPad for school use. I hold up my notebook before swapping it with the iPad in my bag. "I was actually going to use a *notebook* to take notes. Silly me."

Alex chuckles as he powers up his own device. "Here's what I don't get." He glances up at me, dimple flaring in his right cheek. "I mean, if you're going to be sitting *right* in front of me taking notes, why wouldn't you just e-mail me the file? Just seems to make more sense, right?"

I cock my head and smile. "I'm not taking notes for you."

Then Alex stares at me for a minute, all thoughtful like, like he's seeing me for the first time that day. My flat-ironed hair, carefully made-up eyes, and the brand-new sundress/cardi combo I wear with my own designer flip-flops, just because *everyone* is wearing this brand of designer flip-flops.

And in case I haven't mentioned it, I greatly prefer not to stand out. Even if I think sixty dollars is a ridiculous amount of money to pay for rubber shoes.

"Hey, you look really nice today. I like your hair like that."

"Nice try. I'm still not taking notes for you," I repeat, turning around as I notice Mr. Carr working on projecting the syllabus onto the screen of the smartboard.

I stare down at my desktop, taking a deep breath to steady myself, unnerved by Alex's compliment. He offered it so easily, like it's something he would say to anyone. Like there's no reason he should hesitate at all in complimenting me, because after all, we're just friends.

Like last summer wasn't last summer. Sure, all last year, we managed to ignore it. But now it feels like the night of the staff party has been ripped right out of our own personal history text.

Mr. Carr continues to have technical difficulties, and I brace myself and spit the question out without bothering to turn around. "How come you didn't tell me about Leighton?"

Because someone has to acknowledge her, for crying out loud. If we are actually going to go on being, you know, friends.

I hear his breathing catch and then nothing but silence. I have to turn around and confront the topic head-on, even though I really don't want to. Only he's not looking at me anymore.

"C'mon, Jordyn," he mumbles, tracing mindless patterns on his desk with his fingertips.

"C'mon what?"

His fingers still and finally he looks up at me. His eyes are hesitant, expression unguarded, and for just a second we're not pretending. No one's forgotten about last summer. "It feels weird to talk about it with you. I just . . . couldn't."

Everything feels like it's unraveling at once, and way too

quickly, so I force a bright smile and shake my head. "We talk about everything, Alex. When did you two start . . . whatever?"

Alex rubs at his jaw, uneasy, and can't hold my gaze as he answers. "We're working together on the Athletic Council. Because I'm captain this year, I'm automatically on the committee. So after some of the meetings in August, we just ended up hanging out. People were always over at her house, swimming and stuff."

Something inside of me crumbles, because Alex has never hung out at my house and probably never will. I hope the internal demolition isn't written all over my face.

"Oh. That's cool. Sounds like you had a fun end of summer."

Then he's looking right at me again, like maybe he doesn't buy a word of it, but luckily Mr. Carr has had a breakthrough and clears his throat to get the attention of the class. I whirl around like the model student I am, relieved the conversation is out of the way, convinced I was convincing.

Even though I'm used to working nine to five during the summer and heading straight to practice afterward, I feel ten times as tired as I did last week with the prospect of hockey practice looming. My feet drag and my shoulders are slumped under the weight of the textbooks in my book bag as I head toward the locker room to change for our first after-school practice. I drop my gym bag on the bench next to Erin's and we exchange nothing but weary hellos as we change into our sports bras, gym shorts, T-shirts, shin guards, and cleats.

The senior girls are a different story entirely. They emit a frenzied energy as they call loudly to each other across the room, laughter and snarky comments about butt size echoing off the open lockers and cinder-block walls. They're pumped for the season, and locker doors are slammed, shoes are knotted hurriedly, and hockey sticks are tossed jauntily over their shoulders as they try to get down to the field as quickly as possible.

Their energy is just as palpable on the open field as it was within the confines of the locker room. Leighton, standing next to Dana, bounces on the balls of her feet as she waits for the rest of us to assemble in a circle around her to stretch. She pulls an arm across her chest and rolls her right ankle at the same time, and we follow along, a group of compliant mirror images.

"Listen up, you guys," she begins loudly, waiting for all other conversations to end. She stares pointedly at two fellow seniors who don't shut their mouths quickly enough. "Summer was fun and all, but just to remind you, as of today, the season is officially underway." She glances toward our coach, who is halfway across the field, setting up orange cones for a drill. "Time to cut the bullshit," she says firmly. "We have T-E next week, and I will *not* let them embarrass us this year. That cool with everyone?" Without waiting for a response, she gives her next command. "Switch."

She promptly pulls her other arm across her chest and begins rolling her left ankle, and we all follow along, like clockwork. Leighton assesses us and nods her head approvingly.

I drop my head, pretending to stretch my neck, and try to stare without being seen from under my overgrown bangs. Leighton is so comfortable there, the literal center of attention, a group of nearly thirty girls mimicking her every movement. Her position does not cause her to tug self-consciously at the bottom of her tiny shorts or lead her to fiddle nervously with her ponytail. She is supremely confident, reminding me of a lioness governing over a pack.

Leighton and Dana lead us through the routine, and then we jog over to the other side of the field to join Coach Marks. She leads us through a series of drills—dribbling, passing, and blocking. We practice taking shots on the goal from the edge of the circle. We practice penalty shots from mere feet away. Then just before she lets us break for water prior to our daily scrimmage, she sets up a final drill. We are divided into two lines, and when the ball is tossed toward the net, one person from each line sprints toward it, attempting to beat the opponent from the other line, capture possession of the ball, and move toward the net to score.

Slowly, I join the left line, feeling a slight, silly nausea in the pit of my stomach. I hate face-off drills. I hate them more than anything, especially since most of the senior girls have ended up in the other line and I'll likely be paired against one of them.

As my turn approaches, I count quickly, and my stomach does another series of turns when I realize I'll be forced to compete against Leighton for the ball. She will win. Where I'm precise, she's fast. And ultimately, she is more aggressive than I will ever be. I'm not naturally aggressive, and on the hockey field, that makes the difference between mediocre and really spectacular.

Coach Marks blows her whistle and Leighton takes off like a hunter, charging in my direction like I'm the prey. I make a halfhearted attempt to force her back into her space, but fear holds me back.

What happens if I actually beat her? What then?

Leighton doesn't really handle defeat well.

In the end, I'd rather be subjected to her self-satisfied smirk than a glare of annoyance-tinged anger.

Thwack.

The ball hits the net and there it is—the grin, the one that says she's a winner and she knows it. The grin that keeps me in my place.

We run through the drill a few more times, but thankfully the numbers are uneven and I don't have to face off against her again. JV scrimmages varsity, and then it's my least favorite part of the practice—wind sprints first to the twenty-five-yard line, then to the fifty, and eventually all the way to the hundred. We take off to the staccato blasts of the whistle until my calves are cramping and I bend over from exertion, all the while knowing that makes it even harder to breathe.

Finally, mercy is granted and I hobble toward the bleachers. Leighton reminds us we need to stay for a minute so she can dole out our uniforms in time to wash them before the game next week. She hands out maroon away jerseys, white home jerseys, and maroon-and-charcoal kilts. Leighton and Dana check the numbers on the shirts to make sure the captains, along with their closest friends on the team, get their numbers from last year.

Leighton retrieves the next shirt from the box; it has the number twenty-three on the back. She stares at it a moment, then rolls her eyes. She scans the crowd until her gaze, still entirely unamused, meets mine. The jersey is tossed in my direction, with much more force than necessary. "Alex said to make sure to give you number twenty-three." She shakes her head. "I don't really get the inside joke . . . but whatever. The number's free, so there you go."

"Thanks," I mumble, folding the shirt neatly to busy my hands. The idea of my having an inside joke with her boyfriend seems to have irked her. I don't smile at the idea of Alex telling her to give me a certain number or the image of him laughing as he imagined how annoyed I'd be at one more M.J./twenty-three reference.

Leighton has just added a new layer of worry to my concerns about the status of my friendship with Alex. This morning, I was forced to acknowledge an unexpected distance between the two of us. Now, it occurs to me there might also be an actual barrier between me and Alex, a person who is interested in keeping me from closing that distance.

When we're dismissed, I shower quickly and stumble to my car, completely disheartened, already feeling the lactic acid accumulating in my muscles. I can imagine how sore I'm going to feel by the time I get home and have to stand up again. It's been a long-ass day and suddenly I feel more exhausted than ever.

Chapter Two

By five forty-five on that first Tuesday of the school year, all I want out of life is a Pablo & Pancho's chicken enchilada.

My mother and I go out to eat at my favorite restaurant every year on the first day of school. It's rare that we eat out during the week; in fact, it's rare that my family goes out to eat at all. This is something special for *me*. Another rarity. Most weeks, days, minutes in the Michaelson household revolve around my brother, Phillip. But I don't usually complain, at least not out loud.

Fair doesn't mean equal, fair means everyone gets what they need.

It's a concept that's been drilled into me since I was three years old. Phillip needs a lot more than I do and any equitable division of time, attention, resources, or preference goes straight out the window in my parents' attempt to apply this concept of fairness.

But on the first night of the school year, it's my turn to come first for once and I look forward to our trip to Pablo & Pancho's after a month of at-home meals during August. It's not only the melted cheese I'm craving. It's nice to have my mom's undivided attention for a couple of hours.

I know my mom looks forward to this night, too. I usually find her waiting eagerly at the front door, lipstick freshly applied, dressed in a pair of reasonably fashion-forward jeans. (My parents really don't get out much.)

But when I walk in the door, I find Phillip instead, hooked up to one gaming system or another, headphones on. He makes happy little grunting noises and occasionally flaps his hands at his sides. My arrival doesn't even register on his face, flashing with the bright colors from the screen.

I stare at him for a minute. It'd be easy enough to ignore him—he prefers to be ignored. But every once in a while, Phillip checks back in to the human world and there are these moments of clarity. He sometimes says my name, reminding me that he actually knows it. He might look right at me with those shocking blue eyes. Puzzled expression on his face, he might ask, "Will you help me?" as if he actually wanted someone to take his hand and guide him out of the confusing maze of existence he's typically lost in.

So I sigh, let my hockey-stick bag slide off my shoulder, and approach my brother, even though I really don't have the energy for this right now.

Dropping to my knees in front of him, I wait for eye contact before speaking. I would take his headphones off, too, but that would drive him berserk. Instead, I smile and wave. "Hi, Phillip. How's Phillip today?" Pronouns don't make sense to Phillip.

He grants me eye contact for less than three seconds before returning his gaze to the screen. Then he laughs maniacally. "Aww, cheer up, Squid, it could be worse."

"Phillip, look at me. Look at Jordyn."

"It could be worse." He laughs again. "It could be worse."

Bizarre as they are, something about his words actually resonates, given the day I've had.

I grit my teeth and stand, quads screaming in protest. It's not a clarity kind of day, apparently. Phillip's not in Berwyn, he's in Bikini Bottom with SpongeBob SquarePants and crew.

I stare down at Phillip's shaggy hair, typically overgrown because haircuts are a battle. My brother is fifteen years old. We are only nineteen months—yet entire decades—apart. I guess he's considered a high school freshman, but he's been in an ungraded program for so long now, the term doesn't really apply.

Phillip's autistic.

If you Google "famous people with autism," the search engine will produce names such as Mozart. Daryl Hannah. Andy Warhol. Even Albert Einstein, for crying out loud. If you didn't know better, you might think that most people with autism are brilliant, accomplished, interesting, even glamorous.

My brother's not really any of these things. He's smart, I have to give him that much, and apparently he's really good at math. He's not sitting around testing advanced mathematical theory like Matt Damon's character in *Good Will Hunting*, though. Most of the time, Phillip does everything in his power to stay in his private little world—as distant as possible from the rest of us— as parents, teachers, and therapists do everything in their power to drag him out of it. It's a mental battle that sometimes turns physical as he fights their attempts.

If Phillip had his way, he'd sit around in his Bose noise-reducing headphones, watching episodes of *SpongeBob SquarePants* on repeat and reciting his favorite lines for hours afterward. He just wants to be left alone, because something about his neurological makeup leaves him unequipped to deal with the sights, sounds, smells, and touches of our human world.

I don't know how well equipped the rest of us are, but a lot more so than Phillip, I suppose.

My mom comes in from the kitchen and right away I know something's up. She's wearing her best fake-cheerful smile. Over the years I've become Pavlovian conditioned to fear the bad news that will inevitably follow. "Thought I heard you! You all ready to go? Taco Tuesday!"

Huh. Maybe no bad news after all.

"Yeah, I showered in the locker room so I'm ready."

She picks up her purse. "Great."

I smile and my stomach growls in anticipation of my chicken enchilada.

Then my mom walks over to Phillip and gently removes his headphones, something only she can get away with. "Come on, Phillip, time for dinner."

My hand freezes on the doorknob. "Umm, where's Dad? It's supposed to be Girls' Night."

Phillip is *not* coming with us. That's not part of the plan.

My mom refuses to meet my eye as she quietly prompts Phillip to shut off his game. Then she says, "Dad messaged me a few minutes ago. He said something came up that he had to deal with immediately and that he wouldn't be home in time to stay with Phillip. There's no reason he can't come with us. We can still do our thing."

I tilt my head and give her a Look until she finally glances over her shoulder at me.

"C'mon, Jordyn, this is the best I can do."

The best she can do kind of sucks. Going out to dinner with Phillip definitely sucks.

I step away from the door. "We can just go another night. Sounds like that will be easier for everyone."

"No, this is our tradition." She stands and puts her hands on her hips. "It has to be tonight. It'll be fine."

Maybe it will be fine, but it won't be good. But she's already busy gathering Phillip's things, double-checking that we have everything he'll need just to get through the meal, periodically prompting and reprompting. "Time for dinner, Phillip. Time for dinner."

"No McDonald's!"

"No McDonald's, Phillip. The restaurant will be quiet."

"No McDonald's!"

"No McDonald's, I promise."

"Vacuum?"

"I'm sure the restaurant has a vacuum."

I roll my eyes and open the door, conceding defeat. Dinner is happening and now I sort of want to get it over with as quickly as possible.

Phillip rides up front because he gets carsick. I'm stuck in the back, getting passing smiles from my mom in the rearview as she tries to concentrate on the road while at the same time keeping Phillip from reprogramming the radio station presets. At least it's a short drive to the restaurant and we make it there unscathed.

The interior of Pablo & Pancho's is dark and cozy, with bench seating and overstuffed pillows, small candles flickering in red-and-blue mosaic cups. Despite the dim lighting, I can still feel the weight of the stares as soon as we walk through the door. Phillip is thin and frail. He walks like an agitated heron, on the tips of his toes, head moving from side to side, scanning the room for something to set him off. My mom actually dangles his Nintendo 3DS in front of him like a carrot but she insists he keep his headphones off until we're seated, why I don't know. He stands out without them.

In the small lobby, mariachi music, rife with the rapid-fire strumming of guitars—"*Ay, ay, ay, ay, ay, ay mi amor, ay mi morena!*"—blasts over the speakers. Phillip claps his hands over his ears and begins shrieking loud enough to drown out the repetitive, passionate refrain of the song. His shrieks are high-pitched and alienlike, but nothing like the full-on screaming that will follow if we don't get him away from the speakers pronto.

My mom quickly guides him to the hostess stand. "Three of us for dinner, thank you."

Phillip grabs on to the tail of the young hostess's shirt as we follow her toward the back of the restaurant, garnering more stares as we go. "Vacuum?"

"Phillip. No touch," my mom scolds firmly, like she's talking to a toddler, not a boy who's taller than she is.

Arriving at a table, the hostess remains polite, but I can tell she's uncomfortable. "I'm sorry?"

"Dyson. Hoover. Eu-re-ka, I've got it!" Phillips thrusts his fist into the air and repeats his little chant in singsong. "Dyson. Hoover. Eu-re-ka, I've got it!"

Mom laughs pleasantly, like it's actually funny. "Phillip loves vacuum cleaners. He's asking what brand you have here."

The hostess smiles brightly, but obviously she thinks we're straight out of the loony bin. "I'll be sure to find out for you." She drops the menus in a messy pile on the table and hightails it back to the hostess stand.

Her answer isn't good enough for Phillip, who's intent on finding the vacuum. My mom struggles to power up his 3DS while using one arm to keep him from escaping the booth. "Dyson. Hoover. Eu-re-ka!" He bounces up and down on his knees and flaps his arms in excitement.

I pick up on waves of annoyance crashing in our direction and trace them back to an older couple trying to enjoy a quiet meal at the table across from us. They scoot farther toward the side wall, as if they wished they could crawl inside it. Away from us.

The restaurant manager approaches from the storefront, where he's been in whispered conference with the hostess. "Welcome to Pablo and Pancho's. My name's Eric, I'm the manager. Just wanted to welcome you and I hope you have a great dining experience this evening."

He's not here to welcome us. He's trying to determine if my brother is the harmless type of crazy or the truly dangerous type.

"Thank you. He won't be any trouble," my mom insists, even as she tugs on Phillip's arm to keep him from crawling over the table.

"Hoover. Dyson. Eu-re-ka, I've got it!"

"If you could possibly just tell us what vacuum cleaner brand you have here, he'll settle right down."

Sure. A perfectly normal request.

But the manager indulges us. "I think it's a Shark."

"Duunnn dunnn . . . duuuunnnn duun . . ." Phillip starts up with the *Jaws* theme song, using his fork and spoon as percussion instruments. "Duuunnnnn dun dun dun dun dun dun dun dun dunnnnnnn."

I hide my face behind the enormous menu, scanning the list of sixty-four combination options as if it were the most fascinating thing ever. One chicken enchilada and one soft taco. Three soft tacos with rice and beans. Two chicken taquitos and one burrito.

I kind of want to crawl inside the wall myself.

Blessedly, I hear the start-up music from the Nintendo player and finally he is quiet.

Our waitress swaps places with the manager, who scoots away in a hurry. "Hi there, I'm Ashlyn." She sets down the complimentary basket of chips and salsa, which I'd normally dig into, except I've sort of lost my appetite. Ashlyn nods toward Phillip. "He's adorable!" she says, artificial smile stretching her cheeks, her reluctance to take our table still visible in her eyes.

The lengths some people will go to work a tip.

"You know what you want, Jordyn?" My mom closes her menu without even looking at it.

It's not usually hurried like this. Usually we gorge ourselves on two baskets of chips and salsa before even ordering and I get a virgin strawberry margarita with a sugar rim. We make it a celebration. But not tonight, apparently.

"I'll have the chicken enchilada combo," I tell Ashlyn.

"I'll have the same." My mom is riffling through the small cooler she brought along, the one that contains various items from Phillip's gluten/casein-free diet that is designed to keep his behavior from getting any *worse*.

She's not paying attention. She always gets the taco special. She doesn't even like chicken enchiladas.

"And I know it's asking a lot," she continues in an apologetic voice, lifting a container of gluten-free mac and cheese from the cooler, "but is there any way you'd be able to microwave this in the back? Maybe just for forty-five seconds or so?"

"I'm so sorry. I'd be happy to, but there's a 'no outside food' policy in the kitchen."

"Maybe a bowl of hot water I can warm it in then. That'll do. Thank you."

It's not like Phillip's going to eat it anyway. He's just going to play with it, rolling the sticky macaroni between his fingers, enjoying the sensation.

After Ashlyn collects the menus and leaves, my mom hands a bag of rice crackers to Phillip, who is happily tapping away at his DS. *Finally* satisfied that all his needs have been met, she dips a chip into the salsa bowl. "So how was practice today?"

"It was okay. Just tiring. It's hard getting back in the swing of things."

"It's a long day for you." She smiles. "No more cushy pool-side job."

"I know, right?"

She's joking, but I've gotten the sense she didn't totally support my decision to work at the snack bar instead of the day camp where I'd worked last summer. But last summer and this summer were two different things. I thought maybe a new position would help me remember that. It didn't really work out too well, even though I'd never admit it to her. Handing out freeze pops just wasn't fulfilling. I missed the campers a lot and I felt jealous of the counselors who received their hugs in my place.

I missed a lot of things about last summer.

"Do your friends have some of the same classes as you do?"

"Yeah, Erin and Tanu are in my English class again. And Alex and I have history together."

"How's Alex doing?"

My mom has never met Alex, but that doesn't mean she's never heard his name. Over the past year, I've found myself talking a lot about "my friend Alex," even when I've made a conscious effort not to.

"He's good." I fiddle with a chip, breaking it into a million little pieces. I stare down at the cheerfully tiled table. "He and Leighton—you know, from the team? They started going out, I guess."

"She seems like a nice girl." My mother crams another chip into her mouth and nods. "Very mature. Always makes a point of talking to the parents after games."

My heart sinks, hearing one more person sing Leighton's praises. I look out the window and my throat tightens. For a moment, I consider sharing my confusing feelings with my mom, hating how they feel all bottled up inside.

But it's not the time to start a real conversation, not with Phillip here. She won't be listening, not really. There's no guarantee we'll actually get to finish talking about anything.

Our food arrives quickly, along with a bowl of hot water to heat Phillip's meal, and without conferring on the matter we both start shoving food into our faces. Phillip's countdown-to-meltdown timer isn't visible and it could expire without warning.

And even though we eat quickly, we don't eat quickly enough. Every now and again my mom drops her fork and tries to cajole Phillip into eating the mac and cheese she went to such lengths to warm. Each time, Phillip shoves her hand away in irritation without even looking at her. Eventually he's had enough of her pestering and lets out a noise that's a cross between an irritable humpback whale and a bellowing moose. The old woman beside us startles in her seat.

Phillip ceremoniously dumps the entire container of mac and cheese onto the table. Then he begins flicking noodles out of his way like he was playing a game of tabletop football. He's telling my mom there's no way in hell he's actually eating it, but what he actually yells is "Holographic meatloaf? My favorite!"

Flick.

A cold, wet noodle flies through the air and lands on the woman's plate. She and her husband both stare at us in horror.

"Phillip! All done."

My mom's voice is stern and she grabs Phillip's wrist, but he twists away from her, pushes onto his knees again, and steps up the game. He grabs a handful of his dinner and throws it toward the couple. His voice grows louder. "Holographic meatloaf? My favorite!"

The couple picks up their plates and carries their glasses to a table far, far away, without even bothering to ask Ashlyn if it's okay. At the same time, my mom flags her down and asks to have our dinners wrapped. Without consulting with me first. I glower down at my untouched second enchilada, biting back "I told you so." Styrofoam containers are packed, Phillip's belongings are gathered, and we're both whisked out of Pablo & Pancho's faster than you can say "bean burrito."

On the way home, I sit with my arms crossed in the backseat, sullen. So stupid. I mean, a restaurant is supposed to be something you enjoy, not something you endure. This is why we default to takeout so often. We should have held out for another night. Now our tradition is ruined. I'm not going to say so to my mother. I'm not going to say *anything* else to my mother tonight. I plan to let her know how I feel by storming up the steps to my room.

But I don't get the chance to disappear in a huff. When we open the front door, we find my dad pacing back and forth in the foyer. His shirt is untucked, his expression is tight and agitated, and his phone is in his hand.

"What's wrong, Jack?"

Phillip escapes to the living room, oblivious to emotional climates, but I wait at my mom's side.

My dad pushes at his eyebrow and looks back and forth between us. He's debating whether or not to answer in front of me. Eventually, he does. "I got an extremely upsetting phone call today."

It has something to do with Phillip, I think at once. It does not cross my mind to consider that anything *other* than Phillip might be wrong . . . how twisted is that? There are grandparents who could be sick, jobs that could be lost, world catastrophes that could happen. But I'm sure it's Phillip. It's always Phillip.

"From the director of Bridges," my dad continues.

Yep. Phillip. Knew it.

Bridges is this super-exclusive school our district pays for Phillip to attend so they don't have to deal with him in any of *their* schools. It has this insane wooded campus complete with a horse farm and state-of-the-art gym with an Olympic-size swimming pool, which warrants the nearly seventy-*thousand*-dollar tuition it costs to send him there each year.

I've attended—well, I've been forced to attend—events there, and it's a pretty cool place. Phillip doesn't stand out among his fellow students, and he seems fairly content to be there. You can tell that his teachers and therapists are there because they want to be, and they don't look at Phillip or talk to him the way the rest of the world does.

I hope he hasn't blown his opportunity to be there.

"Did something happen today? They usually call me." My mom frowns. "I don't think I missed a call." She scrolls through her missed-call list.

What did he do now? Phillip has already had some really rough days at school; what could he possibly have done to cause this reaction from my father?

"Bridges is closing," my dad explains bluntly. "Some serious funding issue, something they thought was going to be resolved by the state in the nick of time." He sighs in defeat, smoothing his hair across his bald spot—his nervous tell. "Well, it wasn't, and effective immediately, they have to shut their doors."

Mom's purse falls to her feet with a thud. "This just happened overnight? There's nothing else anyone can do? And this is the first we're hearing about it?"

"The director was extremely apologetic and is incredibly upset himself." Dad glances worriedly at me, something I don't understand. "But it sounds pretty final."

"So he just has to stay at home now?" I ask.

It doesn't seem right, but I guess we can make do. My mom gave up her job years ago; it just didn't work out, having to leave in the middle of shifts to pick Phillip up from school when he still went to public school and had nearly daily meltdowns.

"No, I was in touch with the district right away. They're adamant that they'll find another placement for him," he explains. "Legally, they have to, within sixty days. I double-checked with an attorney, too."

"That's better news." My mom's shoulders relax. "That there's some guarantee he'll end up somewhere that's appropriate."

But my dad has not relaxed at all. He stares nervously at my mother, trying to convey something.

"The district will take care of it, right? It's not on us to find a new placement?"

"Yes. The director of special education promised she'd take care of it, within the allotted sixty days." He shoots another worried look in my direction as he mentions this sixty-day time frame again.

I don't get it, all things considered. They've received worse phone calls. "That's a shame about Bridges," I acknowledge. "Shame he has to start somewhere new. But there's got to be other options around here, right?"

My dad nods. "There are other options, yes. I can think of a few off the top of my head from when we looked around. But . . ." He looks at my mom again, eyes worried.

For one last, blissful moment, I am entirely oblivious. For one final second, I believe this has absolutely nothing to do with me.

That second passes. My memory of this day will always be divided around the moment before my father breaks the news and the horrible moments after.

"Legally, the district can't allow Phillip to sit at home," my dad explains. "Legally, until a new placement is found, he has to be somewhere." He steels himself, squaring his shoulders, and finally meets my eye. "They will be creating a temporary education plan, outlining placement in a district program."

District programming doesn't work for Phillip. It never has.

"Thank goodness that's not their permanent solution," my mom grouses.

"So he's going to go to Park for a while?" I ask. Park is the other high school in my district, where most of the special ed classes are located.

My father clears his throat. "There are space issues at Park. Apparently, they already had to set up a whole bunch of modular classrooms because of the size of the freshman class this year. So what they plan to do is set up a temporary classroom for all students from the district that are coming back from Bridges until their new placements are found." His eyes cloud with renewed worry. "Jordyn, honey, they're setting up the classroom at Valley Forge."

My breathing cuts off.

Valley Forge. As in my school. As in . . . no. *Just no.*

My nails cut into my palms as the words escape from my mouth. "No. Absolutely not. That's not a solution." I fold my arms across my chest.

My mom's face is twisted with concern but her words offer little comfort. "I'm not sure it's really up to us, honey. All we can do is get moving on this as fast as we can. I'll pound the pavement, speed the application process along the best I can. We'll get Phillip in the door somewhere that's right for him. As soon as humanly possible." She inhales sharply. "But, no, we can't make that happen overnight. We'll just all have to deal with this for a little while."

"No," I repeat. Salty, frustrated tears coat my throat as I remember the very recent scene at the restaurant, and I struggle to speak around them. "I don't care if it's ten days, I don't care if it's two days. One day is too much." I suck in a shaky breath. "It's not *fair*."

It's not. I cannot deal with Phillip at school. I can't take the whispers and stares, having them turned in *my* direction once everyone realizes what Phillip's last name is.

For once, my parents have the decency to refrain from defining the concept of fairness for me. But that doesn't mean I get off entirely lecture-free.

"Jordyn, this is hardly ideal for anyone," my mom says tiredly. "It's not particularly fair to Phillip or to us as his parents. This last-minute notification is just appalling."

I actually resort to stomping my foot against the hardwood floor. "It's not appalling, it's bullshit!" I yell. "Why did we have to move into this stupid district last summer if this was going to fall through *one* year later? Why did I have to leave the

I went to forever, all my friends, so that Phillip could live close enough to go to Bridges and have a reasonable bus ride? Are you kidding me? It worked out for *one* year and now we're back to the drawing board after changing so much in the first place?"

"You're at a really good school now, a better school," my dad tries to remind me. "There are opportunities for you here as well. You'll have your pick of colleges with Valley Forge at the top of your transcripts."

I shake my head, furious. "Don't act like this move was about me, please, do not *seriously* try to play it like that. If Phillip hadn't needed to go to Bridges, we never would have moved."

Their eyes reveal everything. What I said is true.

"And for the record," I inform them, "Phillip will get eaten alive at my school. Kids will be mean to him. Teachers will be mean to him. Trust me, at my school, you're expected to fit in. You're going to subject him to that?"

My mom rubs at her temples and closes her eyes. "It's temporary. By November, all of this will be over."

"By November, my life will be over! Thanks."

My father's jaw tightens, and I can tell my parents are reaching the point where they will yank me back into line. But before they get the chance to do so, Phillip joins us in the foyer. His hair is disheveled from the headphones and from playing with it and his face is tight with agitation.

"Gary, what are you doing here? You're causing a scene!" he screams. Another stupid SpongeBob line. "A scene, Gary!"

He charges toward me, wagging his finger in my face, because as always, it's all about him.

I never yell at my brother.

But tonight, I do. "I can yell if I want to!" I scream back right in his face, which only makes him scream more, as if he's been zapped with electricity.

I stomp up the stairs, tears of anger and bitterness blurring my vision. It's. Not. Fair.

All I wanted tonight was the chance to enjoy a chicken enchilada in peace.

All I wanted was to be going on with life as I know it.

Everything is changing. And somehow I have ended up on the brink of a disaster, one I can't do anything about.

An hour later, I sit uselessly at my desk, head in my hands. Someone knocks on my door, and my mom doesn't wait for permission before coming into my room. She carries a cup of steaming tea and balances a plate of shortbread cookies on her forearm.

She sets the plate and cup on my desk. "I'm sorry," she says a minute later.

"Stop apologizing," I mumble, staring at the fake wood grain of my desk. "That's not what I want."

I hate when they apologize for Phillip.

She leans in closer to brush the hair back off my forehead. Her voice is less timid this time. "I *am* sorry," she repeats honestly. "I'm sorry that you have to deal with this, too. I'm sorry that our dinner, something I love and cherish, got . . . well . . . ruined. I'm sorry you're feeling so upset right now. You're my daughter, I love you more than anything, and I am so, *so* sorry about these things."

Tears fill my eyes again. "I'm sorry" doesn't change anything. It doesn't make any of this better.

"Why can't he just stay at home till he can go somewhere else?" I whisper in desperation.

My mom perches on the edge of my bed. "I thought about it," she admits, "requesting homebound instruction, or a tutor." She sighs loudly. "But in my heart, I know that if we let Phillip stay out of school for two months? If we give him that out? We'll never get him back, honey. He'd regress a lot."

"And you don't think he's going to regress anyway, making him go through so many changes in two months' time?"

"I'm afraid so. If Phillip ever comes to believe that school is an *option,* he'll go back to fighting having to go with every bone in his body."

Her voice is resolute. There is no wiggle room.

I scratch at my desktop with the empty metal socket where the eraser used to sit atop my pencil, leaving gashes behind. "When is this going to start?"

She takes a deep breath. "Probably by Monday. We need to get him back, somewhere, before he gets used to sitting at home. But I already have a list of four potential schools," she follows up quickly. "It's sixty days, at the most. If one of these schools can take Phillip sooner, the district is ready to move on it as soon as possible, okay? I just need you to hang in for a little while, and this will all be over. Worst-case scenario, it's still only two months."

I try to picture Phillip walking through my school. I think of the pressure us normal kids have to deal with, how it's like a tightrope—balancing, going along precariously without disrupting the flow. Meeting expectations, impressing the crowds.

She doesn't get it. Two months will ruin everything. Two months will knock me right off.

Knock him right off even faster.

There is no sense in trying to make her understand.

"Okay," I mutter, even though it's not okay at all.

My mom stands to leave, leaning down to kiss the top of my head on her way out. "Have a cookie. It'll make you feel better."

"Yeah, right," I grumble.

But the second she leaves, I stuff both cookies in my mouth, barely bothering to chew. And once it cools some, the tea is actually soothing, and for the first time in two hours my head starts to clear.

I notice something sitting on the corner of my desk. It is the first-aid guide from the required summer training at the tennis club. I haven't glanced at it in months, but now I read the first-responder credo on the cover with new eyes.

Thou Shalt Not Panic.

The steps are outlined below: Tame your emotions. Apply logic. Promote positive thoughts.

To me, Phillip showing up at my school is as much of a crisis as anything. I look at the final step to resisting panic. Take charge.

There is no way to make good of a crisis situation. The best I can do is attempt to survive it.

Take charge.

I unzip my book bag and pull out my shiny, blank agenda. I turn to September and find Monday's block. I write the number one in the upper left corner. I count my way through September and October, making a sixty-day timeline. Maybe I will feel better when I see the actual end in sight. This will not last forever, and now I can see that in black and white. I just have to survive it.

I have sixty days. Sixty days to just survive.

Chapter Three

I don't know what I expect to happen on Monday, as I sit in my car until the last possible moment, dreading going to homeroom.

It's not like the initials "P.S." have been stitched onto my jacket, revealing my identity as Phillip's Sister to all. It's hardly like anyone's strung up some banner in the lobby welcoming him to Valley Forge High School. I don't think anyone plans to announce his arrival, but . . . discretion isn't really Phillip's thing.

I sigh and climb out of my car, slamming the door and shaking my head as I walk toward the building. Phillip's transition to Valley Forge isn't my problem. I think it's a terrible idea to begin with, but it's not my job to worry if he'll survive the day. He has a one-on-one aide for that, someone who must have the patience of a saint, who agreed to follow him from Bridges back to district placement.

Her name is Anne. It's Anne's sole responsibility to keep Phillip content and contained, and to keep him from disrupting the lives of others. She maintains his comprehensive binder of strategies and behavior plans. I really hope she's good at her job.

Even knowing that Anne accompanied Phillip on the short bus to school this morning, I brace myself as I walk into the empty lobby, expecting to hear yelling coming from some distant part of the building. Phillip doesn't take to new places and he hasn't been forced to attend school in almost a week. If either of these realizations crosses his mind, I'm sure I'll be able to hear his piercing screams from the farthest point in the school.

In fact, as I stand in the large vacant room, I'm half convinced I *do* hear him, that there's a phantom ringing in my ears I can never quite escape, knowing he's on the premises. Eager for distraction, I scurry toward the wing of junior homerooms. I take a quick moment to give thanks that my part of the building is far, far away from the home economics kitchen, which has been converted into a makeshift classroom for my brother and his few classmates.

But physical distance doesn't grant peace of mind, and I'm on edge all day. Even though I don't spend a single second with my brother, I have the same feeling I do when my family is out in public. Exposed. Vulnerable. On edge. I take long, looping paths around the outer wings of the school, on high alert for the screaming, arriving at two classes late and earning pointed looks from the teachers. It's only the fifth day of school, after all.

I almost welcome our grueling hockey practice. I know that Phillip is tucked safely away at home, and beating my body into the ground provides a strangely welcome alternative to the mental stress I subjected myself to all day.

As I climb back into my car to head home, I notice a bag of

grape Jelly Bellies, my favorite, on the passenger seat. There's probably over ten dollars' worth from the candy store at the mall, where you can scoop your favorite flavors instead of having to hunt for them in the mixed bags. Curious, I open the small tag attached, finding my mom's handwriting inside.

Thanks for "bean" such a good sport about this—your father and I think you're really "grape." It'll all work out.

I grimace and set my gym bag on top of the candy. If she had just left well enough alone, I may have smiled at her stupid pun. But she had to go and add a false promise.

My day had been hell, and all I have to show for it is a single line crossing off *one* day in my planner. One down, fifty-nine to go. This isn't working out at *all*.

Somehow, miraculously, Phillip and I survive our first week together at Valley Forge without any major disasters. (Fifty-three days to go.) Although, the word *together* doesn't really apply. I do everything I can to keep my distance from him, to distance myself from the reality of his presence altogether.

Still, there are a few minor mishaps the second week.

The first almost incident happens on Tuesday afternoon when Alex and I are standing beside our Gifted teacher's desk, looking for a stapler during independent study. I notice the daily attendance sheet that goes out to teachers, listing who is absent, who's coming in late, and who's leaving early. My brother has an appointment with his neurologist this afternoon. Phillip Michaelson. His name is in print, right there, an inch away from Alex's thumb.

I hold my breath, waiting for the inevitable dawning of recognition. The question that will certainly follow. My entire body is tense as I stare at the paper, wishing the name on the page into oblivion.

Alex finds the stapler under a folder, holds it up to me with a smile, and returns to the table. In reality, I doubt he even glanced at the attendance sheet. In the meantime, I'm on the brink of hyperventilation.

The second almost incident occurs on Thursday. I'm standing in the lobby, first thing in the morning, with the entirety of the varsity hockey team. Leighton is handing out "spirit ribbons"—curlicues of maroon and silver to wear in our ponytails—in preparation for our afternoon game. I look up while fastening Erin's ribbon onto her long ponytail and make eye contact with Terry Roth.

Terry Roth is Phillip's Behavior Support Consultant, his BSC, from one of the outside agencies whose goal it is to provide support to Phillip across the home and school settings. Terry Roth has worked with our family for over two years, staying with us even after the move, and she's spent countless hours in our home. But now she's in my school, walking toward the main office, familiar purple plastic clipboard in hand.

She notices me, and a bright smile graces her friendly face as she lifts her hand to wave. Terry knows me well—we're friendly rivals across the board of the special-edition SpongeBob Connect 4 game she bought in the hopes of enticing Phillip into group activities. She changes course slightly, as if she might be coming over to say hello.

But I do not give her the chance. I lower my head, turn on

my heel, and snatch one of the ribbons out of Leighton's hand. I hurry toward homeroom, hastily tying the bow into my hair, ignoring the curious stares from my teammates.

I close my eyes as I walk, trying very hard not to envision the hurt, confused expression that likely replaced Terry's smile.

It's Friday afternoon when the third almost incident happens. I'm not being particularly careful, because it's Friday afternoon and I just need to grab a forgotten textbook from my locker before saying "adios!" to school for the weekend. The final bell has rung and several juniors and seniors are loitering in the junction between hallways, making plans for the weekend.

My brother rounds the corner, heading in the direction of the boys' bathroom, surprising me. Anne trails him closely, ensuring his trip to the bathroom occurs without incident. He is wearing his gym shorts, despite the unseasonably cool fall weather, and his headphones. Even with the headphones in place, I watch as his hands fly to his ears, the noise of other teenagers socializing around him still loud and unpleasant.

Phillip doesn't notice as heads turn in his direction; he never does. He just continues on his course, shaking his head and making little grunting noises as he attempts to block out his surroundings.

I am frozen in place—a deer attempting to camouflage itself among the foliage—as Phillip comes closer and closer.

But there's no cause for my worry.

Phillip's eyes meet mine briefly as he passes, but he looks right through me. His conceptualization of the world is black and white, and to him, Jordyn belongs at home. He does not expect me here, and there is no sign of recognition; my presence doesn't spark the hint of a smile.

A surprising pain grips my chest.

As much as I didn't want my brother to call attention to me . . . it hurts that my brother didn't even recognize me.

I mean nothing to him and have no impact on his world whatsoever. I might as well be another stranger, whose only purpose in life is to irritate him. I might as well be an object.

As I hurry toward the door, I find myself thinking of the pictures in our family photo album, the ones of my nearly two-year-old self seated in an oversized armchair, a swaddled newborn bundle placed very carefully in my arms. In the first picture I'm a combination of petrified and shell-shocked. But in the second picture I'm smiling, bending forward so I can gently plant a kiss on my baby brother's head.

I guess I'd decided pretty quickly that having a sibling might be a pretty cool thing. I guess I inherently knew how to love my baby brother.

As it turned out, I never really got a brother at all. Sometimes being reminded of this can leave me feeling very sad and alone, even when I'm struggling to acknowledge that that brother exists in the first place.

It is Monday morning, forty-six days left according to my countdown, when disaster strikes.

I am unprepared, not expecting it. It's Monday morning, after all, and my guard is down after two weeks of near incidents that never amounted into anything more.

Nothing about the meltdown should have surprised me.

Phillip hates Monday mornings as much as the next person . . . and ten times more than that. After hiding out in our house all weekend, having to return to school pisses him off royally.

Anne is absent, and there is a substitute, a tall, dark-haired male, in her place. Phillip hates substitutes. He hates unfamiliar, unexpected faces barging into his personal space. Men in particular seem to set him off.

And at 10:02, when the hallways are filled with students transitioning between classes, the vice principal decides it's a stellar time for an unannounced fire drill.

Bright red and white lights flash like strobes from the top corner of every hallway. Then there's the noise, a piercing, persistent, drawn-out *bleeeeeeep* that just won't stop. It hurts my ears, it's so loud and unnatural.

Even so, Phillip's screams can be heard above it.

On instinct, I am pulled toward them, even though I should be joining the group of kids filing neatly out the nearest set of double doors.

The screaming intensifies, and I jog toward it, joining the crowd of my peers who have gathered, fire drill ignored, as they all stare, silent and openmouthed, at the display that is my brother. They clutch at their book bags, or cling to the arms of their significant others, half terrified of the crazed animal on the floor before them.

Phillip has apparently thrown his book bag, and books and papers have spilled out of it. He has removed his shoes and peeled off his socks, and as I approach, I see him hurl one of the shoes in the direction of the substitute one-on-one assistant. "Stupid! Dumbass!" The second shoe is thrown. "It may be stupid, but it's also dumb!"

SpongeBob has reemerged.

He yanks at his hair, tugs on his earlobes.

"Stupid dumbass. Phillip goes to Bridges. Put the apples in the basket. THE APPLES GO IN THE BASKET!"

Some of Phillip's rants I can make sense of. I have no idea what the apples are about. The words could mean a million different things or nothing at all.

I end up as frozen and helpless as everyone else.

Phillip wriggles around on the floor as his fight-or-flight responses battle each other. One moment he is curling himself into a protective fetal position, squeezing his eyes shut, clenching his teeth, and stuffing his fingers into his ears. He cries out, as if pained by the flashing lights and relentless noise. The next moment he is lashing out—eyes wild, face red, as he unfurls his long, thin legs and attempts to kick the substitute in the shins.

The one-on-one dodges the blows. I can tell he's trying to maintain a semblance of calm, but his hands are shaking as he fumbles with Phillip's binder, which is way too thick for him to possibly have reviewed this morning, looking for some type of guidance in its pages.

Eventually, he finds some page of instructions and tries to prompt my brother to use his words in a more appropriate way. "Phillip wants . . . Phillip needs . . . ," he encourages.

Phillip retreats and curls back into the fetal position. He is crying again. "My blocks! My blocks! Put the apples in the basket! Why . . . aren't . . . the . . . apples . . . in . . . the . . . basket?" My brother's tears turn hysterical. "Phillip wants blocks. Phillip needs blocks," he sobs.

The substitute's face tightens with frustration. He has no idea whatsoever what Phillip wants or needs.

I do. I can help.

Phillip has called his headphones his "blocks" for as long as he's worn them. It's a term that makes sense to him, I guess, since they do such a good job blocking out all the sounds Phillip tries to avoid. I don't know why he doesn't have them with him for a hallway transition, but the substitute probably didn't have a chance to make it to that page of his binder.

I don't know a lot of things, though.

I don't know why it didn't occur to the vice principal to give a heads-up to the new Autistic Support classroom that a fire drill was coming and that it probably wouldn't be a good idea to be in the halls after third period.

I don't know why I can't move even though I want to.

I don't know why I don't push my way through the crowd and rush to help my brother, as I'm the one person there who knows what he needs. It could be the sheer size of the crowd, nearly thirty juniors and seniors by this point. Maybe it's because I notice Leighton and Dana standing front and center among the group, or because I notice that the surprise and panic has lessened for some, and there are a few people actually starting to giggle. It could be nervous laughter, sure, but it's still laughter.

At that moment, Mr. Daniels, our principal, appears from around the corner, walkie-talkie in hand. He takes one look at my brother on the floor and his eyes widen in shock. He blocks Phillip's body with his, as if everyone hadn't already seen enough.

"This is a fire drill, gang," he reminds us, voice loud and stern. He points toward the EXIT sign. "Outside. Now!"

My classmates duck their heads and shuffle toward the door. I join them, tucking my chin as I go, like someone very purposely avoiding staring at an accident scene as I step around Phillip.

But, keeping an eye out to make sure the principal isn't watching me, I step out of line. I duck into the darkened entranceway to the girls' bathroom and wait.

"I think it's the alarm that set him off," the substitute tells Mr. Daniels.

I roll my eyes. *No shit.*

"Let me run to the boiler room," Mr. Daniels answers. "I can cut the alarm from there." He turns on his heel and strides away.

When he rounds the corner, I spring into action. I'm at Phillip's side in a flash, not bothering to explain my presence or purpose to the one-on-one. I drop to my knees, my own hands shaking as I unzip the front pouch of Phillip's bag, where I know a spare pair of headphones are stashed. They are not as high quality as the Bose pair, but hopefully they'll do.

My brother's eyes are shut and he's still sobbing. If I could, I would wrap my arms around him, or at least squeeze his hand to alert him to my presence. But in such an agitated state, my touch is not welcome. It would pain him further.

I keep my voice even and clear. "Here are your blocks, Phillip. Jordyn's putting on your blocks. They'll help."

I carefully arrange the headphones on his ears and sit back on my heels. His body relaxes minutely, hands beginning to uncurl from fists, the set of his jaw slackening.

Thirty seconds later, the alarm stops. The wide, empty hallway is unnaturally quiet, Phillip's residual cries echoing off the metal lockers.

I start to rise and my brother surprises me by grabbing at my hand. His uncertain, watery eyes meet mine. "Tell Jordyn 'thank you'?"

I hold his gaze and nod quickly, conveying my understanding. Somewhere within his convoluted speech patterns, he is expressing his gratitude.

Before the substitute can ask a single question of me, I am gone, joining the crowd outside as if I'd always been a part of it.

Chapter Four

That same afternoon, I have independent study with Alex.

As I walk into the small room, I'm devoid of the troubling mix of foolish anticipation and faint sadness that I usually bring with me to the Gifted classroom.

Phillip's disability can be a powerful thing, trapping not only Phillip behind its walls, but other people, too. After the fire-drill incident, I feel displaced and distant. Not only is my mind a million miles away, but it feels like my body is, too. My perception of the morning's events, my understanding of them . . . they're so different from everyone else's. As gossip circulates about "the new crazy kid who went psycho in the hallway," it's clear that no one realizes I was involved.

Certainly not Erin, who innocently wondered aloud at lunch if the boy was "crazy, or maybe retarded, or what?"

So when I see Alex already seated at the table, I'm not affected the way I normally am.

He looks up, adorable as ever in a distressed plaid shirt with the sleeves rolled to the elbows, and smiles at once. "Hey, Michaelson. Happy Monday!"

Alex means it to be ironic, but all things considered, I'm not amused.

I mumble a greeting in response and collapse into the chair across the table from him. I pull out my binder, trying to focus. "Did Mrs. Adamson tell you what we're supposed to be working on today?"

He glances across the room, where our Gifted and Talented teacher is running lines with another junior, one who has decided on a first-trimester project of having a successful audition with a professional acting troupe in Philadelphia for the holiday production of *A Christmas Carol*. Pretty ambitious, independent study projects considered.

"She said she really wants our project proposals by the end of the week." Alex holds up his half-completed, stapled packet and grimaces. "I'm trying to take care of the paperwork today so I can get back to actually doing something with the time. Things are getting kind of tight for me."

He's alluding to his Eagle Scout project, which he has been working on as part of independent study since the spring.

I nod, and he asks me, "Do you need a packet? You know what you're going to do first trimester?"

"No." My answer is blunt and crisp. Distracted by Phillip, I've given the topic little thought.

Alex shakes his head and makes a *tsk-tsk* noise. He leans back in his chair and crosses his arms behind his head, which causes his shirt to rise, providing me a glimpse of his boxers above his jeans. I try really hard not to look.

"Not like you, Michaelson," he scolds teasingly. "I figured, if anything, you'd be struggling to pick which of your *five* projects you actually wanted to focus on."

Last year, I did accomplish a lot. I came in knowing the reputation of my school. I felt the need to prove myself, to show that I deserved to be in their prestigious Gifted and Talented program and that I wasn't just "grandfathered" in based on my participation in a challenge program in my old, less rigorous school. I'd written four chapters of a dystopian teen novel and restructured the school's recycling program. All before Thanksgiving.

This year to date . . . I have nothing.

Alex is looking at me, eyes bright, waiting for me to join our familiar banter, our shtick.

When I don't, he leans over and draws a quick cartoon portrait on one of the blank packets. He perfectly captures the obvious tension surrounding me in my features, and even my hair looks on edge. Normally, if it was run-of-the-mill stress I was feeling, his picture would crack me up at once, and I'd feel a whole lot better.

I barely manage to force a smile.

The amusement drains from Alex's eyes. He leans forward across the table, his face serious and concerned. "Jordyn?"

The sound of my first name throws me—it's lobbed above the wall I feel surrounding me and actually reaches my heart.

But I'm not sure I want to feel anything right now.

I stare down at my binder. "Mind's just somewhere else," I mumble.

I make the mistake of glancing up, just for a second, and his eyes are as deep and thoughtful as ever. He looks at me, and he is worried. "Everything okay?"

Teenage guys are not supposed to be concerned like this. They are supposed to tell fart jokes, and comment on girls' boobs, and not really pay attention when something is bothering a friend. It's really, really difficult when they convince you they can be something else entirely—a human being, one who truly cares, *especially* when they're less yours and more someone else's.

Pain nudges at the numbness in my chest.

"Nothing you can fix," I snap.

Alex's spine straightens against his chair as he literally backs away from me. "Alright, that's cool." His voice is tight and flat, matching mine. He bends over his paperwork and busies himself with completing the form.

I take a blank copy and pretend to get to work, too.

Except I have a couple of problems. The first being that I truly don't have a first-trimester project lined up. The second being, I can't stop myself from glancing up at him, every few seconds.

The annoyance has faded from his face. I can tell he's trying to concentrate, but it's obvious his mind isn't really on his work, either. Alex's eyes are drawn and his mouth is cast downward. He looks genuinely wounded, and I am surprised my stupid behavior has this kind of power over his mood.

Alex glances up once, and his eyes hold mine for an extended minute, assessing me, begging to understand the reason behind my snarkiness. It's the look from him that will forever break me.

So I hear myself apologizing. I am in a bad enough mood for the both of us, and he really doesn't deserve the misery.

"Sorry for snapping." I wait for him to look up again. "Really . . . I'm sorry."

His sweetest smile reemerges, and his eyes clear. "It's okay, Michaelson. I told myself I knew better than to take it personally. You girls are moody. I'm learning that quickly." Then the concern flickers in his eyes anew. "You just seemed really upset, but . . . I didn't mean to pry."

I *do* feel bad, but I still don't want to talk about the thing that is weighing me down. So I force a smile, shake my head to dismiss his concerns, and scoot my chair toward the corner of the table, closer to his. "So what exactly do you still have left to do?"

Alex mirrors my actions, scooting his chair closer to mine in return. The butterflies in my stomach flit their wings as I detect the familiar scents of Kenneth Cole Black cologne and cinnamon Trident.

"A lot," he answers. He slides the small crucifix, the one he's never without, back and forth on the thin chain, a habit that emerges whenever he's anxious about something. "It's a damn good thing that Mrs. Adamson gave me permission to work on this as part of independent study, even though it's kind of double-dipping. I know it's been two semesters in a row, but I really need the time."

I shrug. "I hardly think you should feel bad at all about spending your study time to do something so productive." I roll my eyes in jest. "Really puts my recycling efforts to shame, ya know?" He's so close, and I feel brave enough to reach out and touch his sleeve, just for a second. The material is warm and soft against my hand and it's harder than I expect to pull away. "You deserve a lot of credit on all fronts. It's really challenging, but more importantly, it comes from a really kind place."

Alex's heart is truly a really kind place.

A hint of color appears on his still-golden cheeks. "It's not like I'm doing it all alone."

"Yeah, but the project never would have even gotten started without you. It wouldn't exist in the first place."

He chews on his lower lip. "It just better turn out, right?" He laughs, the dimple in his right cheek appearing. "I'm going to be pissed off if this crazy vision I have in my head doesn't pan out." Alex's brow furrows and he sighs as he leans forward. "I spent so much time with research and fund-raising, I'm not sure if there's enough time left for the product to actually come together. There's only about four weeks left until the dedication ceremony."

"How can I help?"

"That depends on how handy you are with a circular saw or power drill," he answers, lips quirking back into a smile.

My eyes widen in terror. "Ugh . . ."

The expression on my face cracks Alex up. "I'm just kidding. There's painting, planting, cleanup . . . lots of things I need help with, actually. I was thinking about sending some sign-up sheets around school, maybe trying to get together a Saturday work session."

"Well, count me in. Provided I can have an exemption from the power tools."

I'm really happy to hear I can help Alex out and show support for what he is trying to accomplish in our township. After realizing there was a dearth of wheelchair-friendly playgrounds anywhere within a twenty-five-mile radius, Alex set out to change that. He tirelessly researched playgrounds for kids with disabilities around the country, spending hours reading product reviews of ramps, elevated sand tables, and wheelchair-friendly swings and seesaws. Then he partnered with a local charity to raise the necessary funds, pounding the pavement with candy sales, car washes, and hoagie sales. Campaigns with local businesses. Donation jars in every store in town.

Alex has finally arrived at phase III—playground construction—and he still refuses to take a backseat to the construction company doing most of the work. To Alex, the project is still hands-on.

He's shared the blueprints, sketches, and equipment images with me, and I have no doubt that the playground will be functional, beautiful, and impressive.

"It's going to be *so* worth it," I remind him.

"I hope so." He fiddles with his paper, flipping it over, back and forth. When he speaks again, his voice is low and shy. "I get so annoyed when my mom has to feel apologetic about not being able to maneuver around somewhere. How she sometimes has to feel like she's an inconvenience to us, for something that isn't her fault at all." He shakes his head. "And she's an adult. Little kids who just want to go to a playground, to have fun like every other little kid, sure as hell shouldn't have to feel that way."

Does Leighton even appreciate you? Does she really? Does she deserve you?

I push the intrusive thoughts from my mind and try to refocus on our conversation. "Your mom . . . wow . . . how proud is she going to be when everything's finished?"

The color flares again in his cheeks. "Yeah . . . well . . . hope so."

Alex's mom is a lifelong diabetic. Six years ago, complications with her condition resulted in a severe stroke at a shockingly young age. As a result, Mrs. Colby's facial features are distorted by partial paralysis, her speech is garbled, and she is wheelchair-bound.

I think the second or third time I acknowledged I was probably in love with Alex was when I saw him pushing her around the tennis club last summer for Family Day. He took such good care of her and seemed so damn proud to be pushing her wheelchair.

Knowing that Alex has a family member with a disability has made me consider confiding in him a thousand times. I'm sure in his home, it's sort of like mine—every aspect of family life revolves around the limitations of someone else in the house. He could sort of relate, right?

But I always decide . . . not really.

Despite her speech problems, Mrs. Colby is *with it*. She is sweet and friendly, a social butterfly that simply lacks wings. She'll talk your ear off when she sees you—even if it takes a while for her to spit it out—and she remembers everything you ever said to her. She enters wheelchair relays and decorates her spokes for the seasons. Blinking pumpkins illuminate her wheels through October and November, then they're replaced with green and red tinsel as soon as Thanksgiving passes. Everyone loves Mrs. Colby, you can just tell. She's hardly a source of embarrassment or pity.

So Alex really can't relate at all.

He's finished filling out his form for Mrs. Adamson and reaches toward the far end of the table for a stack of brightly colored flyers. "If you really need a project idea"—he slides a neon green paper across the table toward me—"here you go."

I stare at the flyer, announcing the regional Oracle Society's annual high-school speech competition, slated to take place at Villanova University at the end of October.

Alex raises an eyebrow. "Bet you could write an amazing speech."

I start folding the paper in half. "Yeah. Too bad there's just that small little issue of delivering it to, oh, what? A few hundred people in a college auditorium? With a panel of judges sitting front and center? Suuure."

Alex's eyes take on that serious cast again. "You shouldn't have let me read the first couple chapters of your book then."

"I didn't!" I laugh. "You took my notebook without asking."

"Either way. Now I know how good your writing is." He taps the speech-contest flyer with his pencil. "Just a shame not to share your words and ideas."

I flip my hair over my shoulder, aiming for glib. "Once I'm a published, *New York Times*–bestselling author, they'll be shared with plenty of people."

I have to laugh at his idea. Public speaking really isn't my forte. That whole "eyes on me" scenario I hate so much. By *choice*.

And before I fold the paper in half, I catch a glimpse of this year's topic.

"The Power of Speech."

Silly thing for me to try to write about. As someone who stays silent about so many things she's thinking, feeling, and enduring, I really have no business commenting on the topic.

Chapter Five

It's a quiet day at school on Friday. (Forty-two days to go.)

I have a successful afternoon. We play a home game against Great Valley, and we win. In my position as midfielder, I don't have a lot of opportunities to shine in terms of goals scored or blocked, but my performance is steady and strong. I set Leighton up for most of *her* goals, at any rate.

The mood in the locker room is exuberant and silly as Leighton and Dana flit through the room, spinning the rest of us in impromptu dance moves and handing out bunches of victory Blow Pops. Sometimes, I'm as susceptible as everyone else, and the positive attention from Leighton feels like a gift.

My family isn't at home—maybe Phillip has a med check with one of his various doctors—and I blare the radio loud enough for the Black Keys to be heard over the running shower. I'm in and out in fifteen minutes, in a pretty darn good mood despite the week's chaotic beginning and excited for the night.

I head toward Bravo Pizza to meet Erin and Tanu for a

brick-oven pie before the football game. By the time we arrive forty-five minutes later, the sun has set and the air is crisp and chilled. Fallen leaves crunch under our feet and I'm glad I dug out my colorful striped gloves to pair with my jeans and long-sleeved field hockey tee. We always wear them after a home win. We make our way to the far end of the home stands, our conversation attempts drowned out by the tinny din of the marching band, the static play-by-play from the announcers' booth, and the rhythmic calls from the cheerleaders.

I spot Alex's mom in the crowd, pom-poms in hand, her wheelchair positioned near the bottom of the bleachers. She sees me walk past and raises her good arm to wave to me. I've only spoken with her a handful of times, but she swore she never forgets a face and she makes good on that promise.

Our group isn't hard to spot, with its members clad in identical maroon T-shirts. We have to sit as a team—Leighton's orders—but at least other friends aren't excluded, so we don't have to ditch Tanu, who would absolutely hate that.

Leighton sits on a fleece blanket in the middle of the group, dressed in Under Armour leggings, gray Uggs, and coordinating maroon headband.

I wonder how it's possible to look so casual and so perfect at the same time.

She turns toward us when we arrive. I notice Alex's number painted on her left cheek and I sort of hope it gets smudged sooner rather than later. "Hey, did you guys get the heads-up?" She jiggles her knees to generate body heat. "Bonfire tonight at the Parish farm?"

We nod in unison, because it would have been impossible to

miss the invite spreading like fire itself throughout the hallways over the past few days.

"Are his parents away this weekend?" one of the other senior girls asks.

Leighton waves her hand carelessly. "No, but it doesn't matter. The fire pit is almost a mile away from the house. There are all those trees. It's not like anyone bothers us back there."

Beside her, Dana smiles and lowers her voice conspiringly. "Good. My sister picked us up a case when she was home last weekend."

Leighton pushes her ear warmers out of the way and actually inserts her index fingers into both ears. "La-la-la-la-la. I can't hear you," she says loudly. "No drinking during season! La-la-la-la-la . . ."

Dana frowns. "But I have a bottle of Goldschläger, too. Your *favorite*."

Leighton huffs and tries again. "No talking about drinking during season. No talking about drinking during season when we are *on school grounds*. Come on, how stupid are you? Coach Marks is probably *here*."

Erin fiddles with her ponytail before working up the courage to interject. "Umm . . . I picked up the stuff for s'mores, too, like we talked about."

Leighton leans down to high-five her. "You're my girl then."

Erin beams like she just aced her precalc final or something.

Then the referee blows the whistle, a frantic jumble pours from the announcers' booth, and Leighton's eyes fly back toward the field. She is on her feet at once, jumping and whooping. "Yeah, Colby! That's you, superstar! Go, *Alex*!"

As he trots from the end zone to the sideline, he removes his helmet, revealing traces of mud on his face. He doesn't turn his head toward the sound of her voice. It was a decent attempt on his part, but he didn't get the first down so the ball is turned over. Alex collapses onto the bench and squirts water into his mouth, which he spits angrily into the grass.

Leighton can't make him a superstar just by calling him one. To me, her enthusiasm is patronizing. And given her display, she's attracted more attention to herself than the person she claims to be celebrating anyway.

We win, capping off a night of Valley Forge victories, from the guys' soccer team to varsity field hockey to the football team. After the adults head out, the school parking lot remains a rampant madhouse. Friends plan to drop off cars and make sleepover arrangements—real and pretend—to appease their parents. Finally, a caravan starts moving toward the Parish farm.

We follow a long, winding path back to the fire pit, where a huge bonfire is already reaching seven or eight feet into the air, licks of flame crackling and escaping higher into the black sky. People are stashing bottles in trunks or arranging themselves on wool blankets or low logs.

It's not long before the smell of pot is wafting out from the grove of trees, and couples, hand in hand, start disappearing into the same hidden area.

Alex and Leighton are not among them. You could almost forget they're a couple at all, the way Leighton is busy holding court among the girls and Alex rehashes the game with his teammates. Occasionally, he makes an effort to catch her eye, and I see him direct his smallest, most intimate half smile in her direction. She looks up and waves hurriedly, barely noticing, as busy socializing as she is.

It's a smile I used to have memorized, one I try not to think about.

I stay with the pack of junior girls, sipping from a Styrofoam cup of hot chocolate that has been spiked with a liberal dose of peppermint schnapps. Erin is managing the s'mores supplies and dunks some extra marshmallows into my cup.

I giggle as I watch them melt, a warm, sweet buzz making a slow path through my bloodstream.

But the groups have started to converge as everyone moves in closer to soak up the warmth of the fire. I pick up pieces of conversation from the members of the football team. Alex's friends.

"The day of the fire drill, you mean?"

"Yeah. Dude, it was fucking nuts."

I know at once what they're talking about and the cocoa warmth in my belly turns ice cold.

"It was kind of hilarious, though," Jason, the quarterback, continues. "It's this skinny, bony kid I've never seen before, chucking his shoes at this big guy who looked like he wanted to run and hide. I'm standing there, like, where the hell am I? Who are these people anyway? I thought it was a hidden camera show or something."

"Ha-ha, it's like in *Austin Powers*," Mitch, a junior player, jokes stupidly. "You know that part? 'Who throws a shoe? Honestly! You fight like a woman!'"

His British accent is atrocious, yet they all seem to find him hilarious.

Even Alex laughs.

I feel blood beneath my cold cheeks. It feels like there is a spotlight directly over my head. It's impossible to stand there and act natural and I feel my mouth twitching as I try to keep my face neutral. But as hard as it is to stand there, it's even more impossible to move.

"No, but seriously," Jason says, "I heard some school for crazy kids closed and they all had to come back to our school."

"For good?" Mitch asks.

Jason shrugs. "Don't know."

Now the girls are starting to involve themselves. "Are they seriously crazy?" Dana questions. "Like, dangerous?"

A hot ball of fury emerges from the cold numbness in my stomach. What a stupid thing to say. Phillip's hardly crazy *or* dangerous.

"I don't know, but I'll tell you this much: That kid was out of control," Jason answers. "He didn't think twice about attacking the person who was trying to work with him."

Attacking?

Phillip didn't *attack* him. Phillip was trying to get away from him, if anything. Phillip was trying to get away from all of it.

"Don't we have a right to know or something?" Leighton questions innocently. "Like, did anyone bother to tell our parents about this? 'Oh, by the by, we're bringing a busful of crazy people into your kids' school.'"

"Course not," says Dana, taking a sip directly from the bottle of Goldschläger. She teeters on her feet. "It's just like all the school shootings. Nobody says anything until after the fact. Then it's all coulda, woulda, shoulda." She giggles, a complete, drunken imbecile.

They don't know him at all. Yet they assume he is crazy, violent. Likening him to a possible criminal, a possible murderer.

Why is everyone always so *damn* stupid?

Hot tears coat my throat and blur my eyes. I need to go. I need to go *now*, or else they might fall, right in front of everyone.

I turn away from the crowd. "I need a minute," I mumble in Tanu's direction.

But she doesn't hear me, and grabs at my sleeve, forcing me to turn around. "What?"

I feel the pressure of unshed tears against my eyes, creating urgency in my escape. "I just need a minute!" I practically shout it, my voice unexpectedly loud and shrill.

Alex's eyes leap up from the ground, finding mine. The laughter drains from them at once, and they are dark and serious, intense with concern, through the fire. I hold them with mine for just a second, begging for the help I can't ask for out loud.

But I have to go, so I turn and stalk off into the grove of pine trees, the ones behind the fire pit, away from the people hooking up or smoking up. I collapse onto the ground on a bed of soft needles that are cold through my jeans. I stretch my shirt's collar over my chin and curl my hands inside the cuffs.

I feel like Phillip, suddenly understanding the desire to escape every single sensation around me.

I glower into the darkness. I mean, truly, I don't really get *why*, when Phillip is so damn distant from me, it feels like any of this is about *me*. Phillip barely exists on the same planet as I do. Besides sharing an address and a kitchen table, our lives rarely overlap.

So why do their comments feel so personal? Why do *I* feel insulted?

Why do they make me so angry?

It's Phillip. Phillip who sometimes doesn't even recognize me outside of our house. They might as well be talking about a stranger.

But . . . they just don't get it. They don't get how much this is *not* a joke.

He's still a person. He's not a joke to share around a bonfire.

My life is not a laughing matter.

Tears finally slip down my cheeks. I draw my knees into my chest and cry into the denim of my jeans. I am silent about it, but I feel the material slowly grow damp against my skin.

When I manage to straighten up, wiping my tears with the back of my hand, I find gray New Balances and a pair of loose jeans in front of me. Looking up, I see the rest of Alex. I didn't hear him approach, and I have no idea how long he's been watching me.

He doesn't wait for an invitation before easing himself onto the ground beside me, Miller Lite bottle in his hand. There is a still-damp quality to him from his postgame shower and he smells like winter, with the smell of fire smoke on his favorite sweatshirt with the Sherpa-lined hood. A particularly rough tackle during the third quarter left a nasty-looking gash above his left cheekbone. The skin around it looks swollen, and for one moment I allow myself to wish I could reach out and touch him.

The moment ends, my fingers dig into my knees, and I stare straight ahead.

He does the same, waiting a minute before asking, "What's eating you, Michaelson?" He takes a swig from his beer.

I clear my throat of residual tears. "It's nothing." I shake my head. "Stupid."

Alex purses his full lips, and then exhales a sigh of frustration through them. "You feel like cutting the bullshit, just for once?"

I turn toward him in surprise. The game has left him *really* surly.

His eyes are so dark and full; I'm not used to seeing Alex like this. He raises his eyebrows, his expression still serious. "You jumped down my throat the other day, in independent study. You never do that. You're staring into space all the time. So . . . why don't you just cut the bullshit and tell me what's going on."

"It's not really the time or place," I stall, chewing on a ragged thumbnail.

Alex glances at our surroundings. "Well, I'm here, so it seems to be an okay place. And I can decide how I want to use my time."

"Wouldn't you rather be out there having fun with Leighton?"

He merely repeats himself. "I can decide how I want to use my time." His voice has an uncharacteristic edge that I attribute to the alcohol. I don't see Alex drink much. "She doesn't dictate everything, ya know, and her little entourage is plenty big at the moment."

Before I can further consider the meaning of his words, Alex nudges my knee with the back of his hand, refocusing my attention. "So whatever it is . . . spill."

I think about how to tell him what's going on while still telling him nothing at all. It doesn't seem like he's going to relent. I poke at the dirt with the toe of my shoe, considering.

"It's just hard," I begin slowly, "hearing people make a joke out of your life. Some things really aren't that funny and sometimes people just have no idea."

Alex's brows are drawn in confusion, but he manages a little chuckle. "Umm, count me as one of those people right now. I don't follow."

I focus on the pressure inside my gut, which has been present since my parents first told me about Phillip starting at Valley Forge. It has been building and building, with the incident in the hallway, with my friends talking about it, with Alex sitting here, demanding an explanation. Sooner or later, I am going to pop. My roiling emotions are reaching a containment limit.

I close my eyes. "So you heard about what happened the other day? What they were just talking about? During the fire drill?"

"Bits and pieces." He shrugs.

"Yeah, well, some kid, one of the kids who had to come back to Valley Forge when a special school closed, he completely lost it and caused a big scene." I bury my chin in the neck of my sweatshirt and tighten my grasp on my knees. My words are barely audible. I can't believe I'm doing this—saying the words out loud—and my heart pounds against my chest in protest. "Some kid being my brother, Phillip."

Alex doesn't even blink. He seems entirely unfazed, but it could just be an act, for my sake. He takes another drink from his bottle. "Why didn't you just say so?" he asks evenly.

"I never say so." I sift through the pine needles with my fingers, letting them fall back to the ground. "Never."

He studies me for a minute, trying to understand something before continuing. "For the record, our friends out there, they're not bad people, right? If they knew he was your brother, they wouldn't be talking like that in front of you."

"Like that's any better?" I ask bitterly. "They might not say it out loud, but they'd still be thinking it. I'd almost rather hear them say it, hear what they *really* think, than have to wonder what they're saying when I'm not listening."

Alex doesn't argue with me but he sits quietly for a few minutes before asking something of me. "How come you never told *me*? I can't believe you never said anything . . . at some point."

He glances toward me and our eyes connect like magnets. I think of the other bonfire we spent together and remember everything. I choke out a weak explanation.

"It's just complicated; everything with my brother is."

"I can't believe it's too complicated to *talk* about," he argues back.

I swallow back my frustration. What's so hard to understand?

"At my house? Phillip defines everything. It's about Phillip, all the time. I get why, sure, but that doesn't mean I don't ever get sick and tired of it being that way." I take a deep breath, which suddenly sounds shaky again. I wait until the trace of tears disappears. "I just get tired. Of being the bigger person, of being expected to deal with it *all* the time, every single day." I shake my head. "Most of the time, I just don't feel like talking about Phillip."

"I understand. A lot of shit's not fair. People take their lives for granted, how easy they can be. You *know* I get that," he finishes, alluding to life with his mother, I'm sure. "What I don't get is why you kept that a secret for over a *year*. At least from me, all things considered. Like, a whole person, you just never mentioned."

"There are lots of reasons why I didn't broadcast the news," I tell him. "Before Phillip was placed in a school that was right for him, he went to school with me, elementary school." My teeth grind together in anger. "You know how in kindergarten, we all knew how to be nice to each other?" I roll my eyes, thinking of the corny analogies teachers used to share, likening different kids to the rainbow of crayons in the box, reminding us we were all different but still all beautiful and special. Then I shake my head. "Well, kids lose that ability really quickly. By about third grade, kids get mean. And they were."

I inhale a deep breath before getting into it. Remembering the story in full, actually feeling it . . . I'm nine years old all over again, confused, and sad, and lonely, and a little bit scared. Scared that something I have no control over can alter my life in a second.

"The older kids on the bus would imitate him. They would whisper or draw back when he walked by. And the whispers weren't just about Phillip. They were about me, too. I can't tell you how many freakin' times I heard 'that's his sister' being whispered when I walked by once people put two and two together."

I shake my head. "I didn't know those kids, so I told myself it didn't matter that much. And I had friends."

Caroline.

I usually try not to think her name.

I remember Caroline clear as day, with her feathery brown hair, blue-gray eyes, and deep dimples. She'd been my best friend since forever.

"But it was, like, one day during third grade, out of nowhere, who my brother was meant something. It meant something bad."

Between kindergarten and third grade, Caroline had spent countless hours at my house. There were sleepovers with Pizza Hut on Friday nights and watching the Saturday morning lineup from our sleeping bags when we woke up. There were fall afternoons spent in my tree house "cooking" meals of leaves and acorns as we played house. Most memories from my childhood involved Caroline.

"One day," I explain to Alex, "my best friend was over during a really bad time with my brother. It got kind of scary, he was really out of control, and she started crying." Caroline actually wet her pants, but I don't tell that part out of some silly lingering sense of loyalty, I guess. "She wanted her parents to pick her up. By recess on Monday . . . everything had changed."

A painful knife slices through me as I remember walking out onto the playground and finding all of my so-called friends whispering under the monkey bars. Caroline was in the center of the group. I smiled as I scampered toward her, but stopped in my tracks at once as I assessed her behavior further. Caroline was giggling and whispering in their ears. She pointedly turned her back to me. Then she wrapped her arms around two other girls' shoulders and led the whole group away from me.

"My best friend actually formed a club against me," I admit. "How stupid and juvenile is that?" I shake my head. "But it wasn't then. It didn't feel stupid. It felt awful. It was the worst thing a girl could do to another girl. They had *rules*, for crying out loud. No one was allowed to talk to me. No one was allowed to sit next to me at lunch. No one was allowed to trade stickers with me anymore."

The tears are blurring my eyes again, even though I'm talking about something as ridiculous as sparkly Lisa Frank stickers, but I don't care. I wrap my arms around my torso, shivering. If it's from anger, sadness, or the cold of being away from the fire, I can't really tell.

"It's how girls hurt each other in third grade," I explain. "I wasn't the first victim, and I wasn't the last. And Caroline, my supposed best friend . . . she tried to act like it was about a million other things. That I'd beat her in the spelling bee that morning. That it was 'annoying' how I wore a ponytail every day. But I knew the truth; I could just *feel it* inside. It was about Phillip. We'd reached a certain age when people were just aware of things, and she didn't want to be associated with my family anymore. Maybe she was just scared, or embarrassed of how she'd acted at my house, or didn't understand that Phillip wasn't contagious or anything, but for whatever reason . . . all of a sudden being Phillip's sister was an unforgivable offense."

Alex remains silent at my side, glaring toward the ground.

I'm glad he's keeping his mouth shut. I'm glad he doesn't have the nerve to act like it wasn't a big deal.

I laugh bitterly as I remember the rest of it. "And you expect adults to set a good example, right? Not so much. That same winter, my mom volunteered to be Cookie Mom for our Girl Scout troop's cookie sale. Except our troop leader, who just happened to be Caroline's mom, came over to ask my mom to 'reconsider.'"

She'd been so patronizing and gentle with the request, acting like it was in Phillip's best interest, how the near-constant ringing of the doorbell and parade of unfamiliar faces would "disturb" him. Really, she just didn't like having Phillip associated with her troop, and she didn't feel like dealing with the fallout. It was easier to exclude us.

Stellar example she set for her daughter.

"Those are just a couple of the stories," I tell Alex, "but trust me, there are plenty. Before I went to middle school, Phillip got placed somewhere else, and when I met a new bunch of kids, without his being on the scene, some of that faded."

I shudder, though, because I never forgot what it felt like. The humiliation and despair of being outcast. The gutting realization that someone I thought cared about me could abandon me over something that had absolutely nothing to do with *me*. It has lingered; it has impacted so many of my relationships, or lack thereof.

"Anyway. I started here last year and no one knew about Phillip. I was just Jordyn. I guess I just sort of liked that feeling. And it's hard to trust that people would be different from what I remember. I decided not to let anyone know that much about me."

The words get caught in my throat and I can't meet his eye, as I reference the building blocks of the wall I put up between us.

Alex tilts his head and I feel him studying me for a long time. "It's a shame you never gave anyone here a chance. Kinda sucks you chose to handle it that way."

My back stiffens defensively. I've always known that Alex would think less of me if he knew the truth. He would want me to be different, better. Braver.

"I'm not a bad person," I protest. "It's just—"

"I know you're not a bad person," he cuts me off. "That's not what I meant."

Seeing me shiver, he shrugs out of his sweatshirt even though he only has a short-sleeved T-shirt on underneath. He drapes it around my shoulders and I am at once enveloped in Alex scent and Alex warmth.

And God does it hurt.

His voice drops to a near whisper and he moistens his lips. "I'm sorry you chose to handle it this way, because it's just really sad to think about you having to feel so alone."

His explanation surprises the hell out of me. It catches me off guard.

My lungs constrict and I can't breathe. My longing is so intense it's nearly dizzying. I want to ball my hands in the soft material of his T-shirt and I want to pull him close to me. I want to bury my face against his chest and I want him to wrap his arms around me. I am longing to be held tightly, I am longing to *not* feel alone.

My fingers inch toward his sleeve, considering.

I force myself to picture Leighton, conjuring up the angry,

determined mask that is her face on the hockey field, charging toward the goal.

She is only thirty yards away, tops. While I sit here, wearing her boyfriend's sweatshirt. What do I think I'm doing?

I already *had* my chance and I blew it. I ball my hand into a fist and shove it inside my pocket.

I ask a stupid question to break the spell. "You're not going to tell anyone, are you?"

It's a ridiculous thing to ask, and he would be entitled not to justify it with a response.

He answers anyway. "No. That's your decision." Alex stands suddenly, brushing off his jeans. "Not my place to judge."

But his voice has tightened and I sense judgment. I do. He thinks I'm a bad person for wanting to keep my brother a secret.

I stare back at the ground. *We're not all as perfect as you are, Alex. We're not as strong or good.*

Ultimately, he finds a small smile for me and extends his arm to offer a hand up. "Come back to the party. I'm sure everyone's moved on."

"I just need a few more minutes. Then I will, promise."

Alex nods in the direction of the empty red cup on the ground beside me, the one I carried back with me. His smile blooms and turns teasing. "You think some of this is just 'beer tears'?"

I can't help laughing; he's probably right. If I hadn't been drinking, I probably wouldn't have gotten so worked up. "Not beer tears, no. But maybe a few peppermint schnapps tears in the mix."

"You guys need a ride later? Andy's driving us."

"Thanks, but we're okay." I shake my head. "Tanu's not drinking tonight. Her mother will be waiting up."

He hesitates, lingering, but eventually concedes. "Alright. If you say so."

Alex turns his back to leave, and my mouth is speaking before my brain grants it permission. I attribute it to peppermint schnapps courage. I could never ask the question face-to-face, but I manage to speak it into the darkness to his retreating figure.

"Why'd you come back here, anyway?"

He stops in his path. He doesn't turn around right away.

When he does, it's written all over his face. There are a million ways he could answer my question, a million things left unsaid.

Eventually, he settles on just one. "You were upset," he says simply. "And look . . . I know there are these . . . boundaries. I know you want them there." He demands that my eyes meet his before he continues, and I know we're not really talking about Phillip or my home life anymore. His expression turns pained. "But you were sad and that makes me sad. I wasn't gonna stay out there and enjoy the party."

He doesn't wait for a response before shoving his hands in his pockets and turning and leaving me for good.

Chapter Six

There's no point in him hanging around, because what am I supposed to say to that anyway?

His words from just moments earlier ring in my head.

"I'm sure everyone's moved on."

This is the truth and about more than a stupid conversation around the bonfire.

Alex has no business hinting at our past now that he's with Leighton. He can't just say these things to me . . . and then walk back to her.

Renewed tears, fueled by frustration and regret, fill my eyes.

The last time Alex and I had wandered away from a group at a bonfire . . . he'd kissed me.

One more secret I never allude to, another reality I keep locked away and closely guarded.

I crane my neck, able to make out frenzied sparks of the fire leaping high into the air between the trees. Then I conjure up the memory of last summer's staff party, which is something I don't allow myself to do very often. If I did, there's no way I could go on being "just friends" with Alex Colby.

The guys from the grounds crew spent a lot of time assisting with the special-needs camp, Camp Hope, which was housed at the tennis club every summer. They carted large boxes of supplies on the backs of their golf carts, manned the grill for us for Friday picnic lunches, and pulled the vans—the large white ones equipped with wheelchair lifts—around front before community outings.

Few of the guys bothered to establish eye contact, their discomfort around the kids with various disabilities pretty obvious. I sensed that they wanted to get off the campgrounds and back to the golf course as quickly as possible.

Alex was the exception.

I noticed him right away, but what girl wouldn't have? Dressed in sneakers, camo cargo shorts, and a gray tank top, his biceps and shoulders tensed and his skin, darkened to the shade of honey, glistened as he toted box after heavy box as we set up for camp. When he caught me staring, he smiled at me for the first time, lifting those beautiful deep eyes in greeting above the top of the box. I think I almost melted into a puddle at his feet, 92 percent humidity notwithstanding.

He tried to pull his chivalrous crap when I followed him back to the van to help with the gigantic boxes of paper towels, but I held my ground and eventually he shook his head and chuckled. I introduced myself, and he assessed me.

"Suit yourself then, Michaelson." He grinned. "Thanks for the help."

I instantly loved the sound of my name leaving Alex's lips.

When we were done, both dripping with sweat, he fished two icy water bottles out of a cooler in the back of the van and encouraged me to sit down beside him on its floor. We exchanged the basics, and then he asked me a more pointed question.

"So you're gonna be a sophomore at Valley Forge," he mused. "How come you're working at this camp and not the other one?"

"What do you mean?" I asked.

He smirked and shook his head. "The girls from school who work camp always choose the 'other' camp. With the so-called normal kids. Then they get to spend most of the day at the pool, and they get to go on better field trips. It's a helluva lot easier, right?" Alex gestured in the direction of the other counselors and administrators working at Camp Hope with me. "Most of the people who want to work at this camp, they're older. More serious."

I didn't have a great answer for him. "I don't know." I shrugged. "This just seemed like the obvious choice to me."

Alex nodded knowingly, like something suddenly made sense. "Oh, so you want to be a special education teacher or something like that? Nurse, maybe?"

I found myself laughing, because I didn't want that at all. "No, it's not that. Like I said, it just seemed like the obvious choice."

I felt his gaze upon me, a mixture of lingering wonder and

maybe a smidge of admiration. But I didn't give him anything else to go on.

The truth I never would have shared is that I liked the idea of being able to reach my campers in a way I couldn't reach Phillip most of the time. As June quickly turned to July, and July melted into August, I was glad I made the decision I did. I fell in love with those kids—the boys with Down Syndrome and their face-splitting grins, the little girl with limited speech who expressed herself instead through her wild, wacky wardrobe, and the kids who were wheelchair-bound but cognitively stable, the ones who never even thought to complain about being stuck in a metal chair all day long.

My campers talked to me, ambushed me with hugs, and even braided my hair. I accepted every touch of their sticky hands, every sweaty hug, and relished their belly laughter in response to my knock-knock jokes.

I could reach these kids, and they reached back. They put a Band-Aid on some type of wound I'd never quite located.

Early in the summer, I was so busy meeting the varied needs of my campers it escaped my notice that one member of the grounds crew spent a lot more time at the camp base than any of the others. He showed no hesitancy in interacting with "my kids," popping wheelies with the campers in wheelchairs, and dropping to his knees to talk to the younger ones at their level.

It was always Alex who helped lower the wheelchair lifts on the vans, and after I commented on how impressed I was with his ability to secure the chairs with such practiced ease, he told me about his mother and why he was so handy in operating a specially equipped van. He relayed her story without a trace of bitterness, then promptly wheeled little Maddie into the van while singing her favorite Katy Perry song, high-pitched and off-key.

I decided if I was interested in falling in love, I would like to be in love with someone like Alex Colby.

I didn't realize at the time I was already more than halfway there.

But I was in limbo last summer, and I was hardly looking for love. I had left my old school but hadn't yet started at my new one. I was still adjusting to the move—new house, new neighborhood, new everything. I was trying to be optimistic, but more often than not found myself teetering back toward resentful about all that newness in the first place. Embracing the idea of Alex, even as a friend, in part meant accepting that the move could be a good thing.

For a long time, I remained shy and reserved, but Alex was none of those things. He grilled me on my tastes in movies and music, my schedule for the fall, and my family. I offered information in bits and pieces, never giving away too much.

One time, while he was busy carrying bales of hay for an obstacle course, he asked another question, all blasé like. "So'd you leave a boyfriend back at your old school?"

I shook my head and mumbled "no" toward the ground. I looked up in time to swear I saw him biting back a smile.

Before long, I was getting personal rides via golf cart back to my car at the end of our long days. I found myself opting to take my lunch break at the same time he took his, "accidentally" stumbling upon him at one of the shaded picnic tables in the grove. We traded our best snacks back and forth like second graders, and on particularly hot, humid days we would sometimes put our heads down, side by side, closing our eyes for a few minutes to regroup before going back to work.

Sometimes I peeked.

It was the one chance I got to memorize his face—the smoothness of his golden complexion, the way his thick black lashes fluttered in rest, and the relaxed set of those perfect lips, closed in a contented pout. Alex was so full of energy and life at every other point in the day, but in those moments he was relaxed and oh-so-close. It was the one time when the idea of Alex wasn't scary, and yet I'd feel my heartbeat vibrating against the warped wood of the table as I stole looks at him.

Then I'd close my eyes again, worried he'd be able to detect my racing pulse, too.

It wasn't long before people started talking. The girls I worked with, most of them in their early twenties with college degrees in education, seemed to get a kick out of us. They elbowed one another and raised their eyebrows when Alex showed up, routinely, on the scene. "We're just friends," I told them.

I kept my physical distance from Alex, trying to send him the same message. That's all it was. I was lucky to have made a friend so that there would be a familiar face when I walked into school in September.

Somewhere, in my heart of hearts, I knew that Alex was anything but.

It all came to a head midway through August, the night of the employee picnic.

The air was thick and shimmering, teeming with humidity and the sound of busy crickets, as we drank frosty mugs of root beer and roasted hot dogs under the heavy blanket of the starry sky. Even though it was nine o'clock at night, we ran to the pool, since we were rarely able to enjoy it without the responsibility of keeping younger campers safe. I allowed myself to get caught up in the fervor, enthusiastically joining in games of Marco Polo and diving for the quarters the tennis club administrators tossed to the bottom of the pool.

Alex was never far, and every time I climbed the steps from the pool, I felt his eyes on me. I was self-conscious in my navy-and-white-striped bikini, but the way he looked at me from the water—eyes dark, inscrutable, and damn near wolfish—almost made the feeling disappear. Desires and urges twisted in my stomach as I allowed my eyes to linger on his, and I dove back into the pool to dislodge the sensation.

When the swimming party was over, we joined the group beside the bonfire where a projection screen had been set up and cones of kettle corn were being doled out. Without bothering to change out of our suits, we wrapped ourselves in the thick white club towels and let our hair dry in the hot night air. Caught up in the magic of that particular night, I ignored the stares of my fellow counselors and sat close beside Alex on an old, worn comforter as the opening credits for last summer's superhero movie rolled.

I blame the mosquitoes for everything that happened after.

They've always been drawn to me and it's never been uncommon for those around me to remain unscathed, whereas I'd walk into the light to find twenty angry red welts up and down my arms and legs.

After listening to me slap uselessly at them for nearly fifteen minutes, Alex spoke up. "That's just a little bit distracting," he whispered with a grin.

"I can't help it! They're awful! I'm getting eaten alive."

"Shhh!" A girl seated directly behind us shushed us.

Alex leaned closer, whispering in my ear, sending an electric tingle down my spine as his warm bare skin met mine. "There's a stash of bug spray in the supply closet. C'mon."

He tugged on my hand to pull me to my feet and I followed him, trying desperately to ignore the knowing giggles that trailed behind us. He held on to my hand longer than he needed to.

When we made it back to the pool deck, the lights had been turned out. The sky had darkened to black velvet, and as we fumbled our way toward the supply closet, which was really a whole supply room, we did so blindly. This time, it was me who grabbed on to Alex, finding his forearm and letting him guide me, certain I was going to trip or be ambushed by a camp of spiderwebs.

He led me into the vast closet. "I know the switch is somewhere on the left wall," he murmured.

The blackness enveloped us, and I swallowed back irrational fear, digging my fingernails into his skin.

Alex suddenly stopped his pursuit of the light.

It all happened so fast.

Even though we couldn't find anything else in the darkness, we had no trouble finding each other. His hands fell to my hips like they belonged there. I felt myself being pressed against the rickety wooden shelves, the firm, warm heat of his bare chest against my damp skin. His breath bathed my face, nervous, and sweet, and excited. Then Alex inhaled suddenly.

I gave in to everything and dropped my hands to his waist. His lungs were expanding and contracting heavily and I allowed my body to melt against his, encouraging him to relax.

When I did, Alex finally lowered his head to kiss me. His lips crashed against mine without hesitation, on the most natural course in the world. They were soft and full and he caught mine between his teeth before softening the kiss and entering my mouth.

My tongue met his, and a ragged noise escaped Alex's mouth and echoed in the darkness. His hands dropped to the bottoms of my bathing suit, and he pulled me all the way against him.

For about two minutes, my walls were down. I twisted my legs around his calves. I pulled him in to me at the same time he pulled me in to him, and I gave up the idea of holding anything back. It was so damn easy in the dark, and for the first time I allowed myself to have something, without considering what would have to be sacrificed or what it meant in the context of my life. For about two minutes, I was honest. I told Alex everything.

But I'd been constructing walls since elementary school, or allowing walls to be constructed around me.

A single kiss, even the best kiss in the history of kisses, was not enough to bring them down.

Something snapped back into place lightning fast, and my stomach filled with panic.

He was too close. He was under my skin.

I was starting over in a new place. And this time around I wasn't sharing my secrets, not with anyone. Not even someone as wonderful as Alex Colby. Especially not with someone as wonderful as Alex Colby. Alex accepted his family as it was, he embraced his mother's challenges. He would think my desire to keep my family life under wraps was wrong. He would expect better of me. I had no desire to be better and ultimately, he'd be disappointed.

I backed out of the kiss, twisting my arm behind me. I fumbled along the panel of the wall, feeling for the light switch. I flipped it on, bathing the both of us in a pool of bright white. Alex stumbled back, as if pained.

His eyes finally adjusted and found mine.

I've never forgotten the sad, confused dismay I found within them. They searched back and forth between mine, and I knew he knew I was gone.

I stared at nothing, a space behind his left shoulder.

"Alex . . . I think it would be better if we were just friends."

He made no further attempt to see anything in my eyes. He cleared his throat, nudging the floor with his foot as he looked down and away. His response was garbled and disoriented. "Wow . . . I'm sorry, Michaelson, I thought . . ."

It was quiet between us for several long minutes before he glanced at me one more time. The question in his gaze felt more like an accusation. He knew I was lying, but he had no idea why. He never asked the question, and ultimately, Alex was the good guy.

He always is.

He straightened up and wrapped his towel more tightly around his hips. I blushed at the sight of him, half naked before me, remembering the longing he'd inspired in me all summer long. "Didn't mean to be a dick," he said, his voice even, constricted. He even extended a hand for me to shake. "So . . . friends?"

I joined my hand with his, still ashamed to look at him. "I'd like that, truly. Friends," I confirmed.

We found the spray and left the closet. But for us, the party was already over.

Sitting in the darkness, staring through the trees at the Parish bonfire over a year later, I remember all of my reasons for acting the way I did, how important and powerful they felt at the time.

But even more clearly . . . I remember what it felt like when Alex held me close. I consider the ridiculous, ever-present distance between us now, and more tears spill down my cheeks. I am so alone, all the time, even when I'm surrounded by people. Sometimes I get really tired of the walls, and I wish I had the strength to just go at them with a sledgehammer.

I try to contain the sound of my tears, because the last thing I want to do is draw anyone else back here.

I shake my head at the shitty irony of it all.

The main reason I pushed Alex away was my reluctance to tell him about my life and my family. Yet tonight, I ended up doing so anyway. If I knew it was going to end up this way, I would have let him keep kissing me that night. Maybe I would have let him stay there, under my skin.

Fear's more powerful than desire, I guess. I'm no braver now, anyway, so it's silly to think about.

I take off his sweatshirt, roll it into a ball, and hide it in the crook of my arm before going back to the party.

Chapter Seven

Even though I know I shouldn't, I pick up Alex's sweatshirt a few times over the weekend. I bring it to my nose, each time half hoping his scent will have faded. But it doesn't, and the *himness* of it is as powerful and painful as ever, instantaneously triggering a visceral sort of remembering and leaving a hollow ache when I stash the shirt away again.

And that's not the only problem with Alex's sweatshirt ending up in my car.

I carry it with me into school on Monday morning, thinking nothing of it other than that I'm kind of reluctant to part with it, a glutton for punishment. I'll give it back to him before homeroom and then I won't have to torture myself anymore.

But I run into Leighton, Dana, and Jamie before I run into Alex. They're standing in front of school because Jamie's on her cell and it's the only place you can get decent reception on campus.

"Hey, Jordyn." Leighton and Dana greet me in passing, barely glancing over as I walk by.

Then Leighton's head whips around as she does a double take, china-doll blue eyes zeroing in on the sweatshirt in my hands. I make myself look much guiltier than I have reason to be, aside from all my furtive sniffing over the weekend, and draw the shirt more tightly against my side a moment too late to make a difference.

Suddenly I'm more than worthy of Leighton's attention. "Why do you have Alex's sweatshirt?"

She hasn't done anything, she hasn't even moved, and yet the chill of fear coats my stomach and I wish I could disappear.

I shake my head, trying to dispel any unspoken accusations. "He just loaned it to me Friday night, at the bonfire. I was cold."

Leighton slowly makes her way over to me. Dana follows, pulled by an invisible string behind Leighton. "Huh. Was wondering where he disappeared to for so long. He left with his sweatshirt on, but when he came back, no sweatshirt." She smiles sweetly, like this is all in good fun, except her smile does nothing to warm her icy eyes. "Any particular reason you're taking off my boyfriend's clothes, Jordyn?"

I try to laugh, but it gets caught in my throat and comes out sounding like pure, choked panic. "Yeah, right." I shrug. "I was upset about something and he knew I needed someone to talk to. He was just being a good friend. He's a good guy like that."

Leighton plucks the sweatshirt out of my arms and hugs it to her chest. "Yeah, I know. I know my boyfriend. I don't really need you to tell me he's a good guy."

"I didn't—"

"I know Alex is best buddies with, like, everyone." She quirks an eyebrow. "But he's my boyfriend now. Maybe I just need to remind him that some things change when you're in a relationship." She presses her lips together and stares at me. "I come first now. I mean, that's the way it should be. It was rude of him to leave like that."

"Yeah. Not cool," Dana echoes. "Of either of you."

"He was just trying to be a good friend."

Leighton tilts her head and chuckles. "I know that. I'm not worried or anything, trust me. He told me you're like a sister or something."

I will my expression to stay blank, desperate for the blow not to register.

"I'm just saying it's sort of annoying, the way he runs around trying to make everyone happy alllll the time."

What's annoying about it? I think. *That's one of the best things about Alex.*

"You can't please everyone all the time," she continues. "I'm his girlfriend and it's not really fair that I ended up by myself for an hour on Friday night while he was being a 'good friend' to another girl."

"I'm sorry," I mumble, dropping my head, coerced into an apology that *really* isn't necessary. She hadn't even paid attention to Alex at the party.

"No worries. It's between me and Alex anyway. Doesn't concern you." A second later, she unrolls the sweatshirt and pulls it over her head. Then she wrinkles her nose. "Eww, do you wear Love Spell?"

I nod.

"This shirt reeks of it. I hate Love Spell. It smells like B.O."

She and Dana turn and walk back toward Jamie without another glance in my direction. Neither one of them laid a hand on me, but I feel as if I've been physically pushed a little farther out of Alex's life. And that maybe I've become more than just a blip on Leighton's radar.

Erin and I have study hall together after lunch. We sit at one of the long tables in the library, and I lean down to riffle through my book bag to find my math workbook. When I straighten, there is a giant flower-shaped sugar cookie, frosted with yellow and green icing and wrapped in cellophane, on the table in front of me.

I glance at Erin, who gives me a small smile. "Where'd this come from?" I ask.

"Panera. I picked it up this morning."

"For me?"

She nods.

"What for?"

Erin clears her throat, fiddling with the strap of her Coach tote. "I heard you were upset on Friday night. I was pretty buzzed, but Tanu told me later. I just . . . wanted to make sure you were okay."

Her brow furrows and she frowns down at the table, as if ashamed. "You listened to me go on and on and *on*, all summer, about Bryce and the breakup. You were forever calling to check in on me, sometimes like you could sense when I was really having a rough time with all of it." Erin looks up again, and

I swear I see a trace of tears glistening in her eyes. "I feel so bad. I didn't even notice when you were upset. I suck."

Oh God. The last thing I want is for Erin to make a big deal about my mini-breakdown on Friday night. I certainly don't want her lack of involvement to be one more thing for her to worry about.

I'd wish the whole ugly incident away if I could. The bitterness over Phillip and the pain over Alex had lingered throughout the weekend. His comfort was fleeting and ultimately drew some very unwanted attention from the senior girls. I don't want to dwell on any of it.

So I plaster a huge smile on my face and roll my eyes dismissively. "Hey." I reach across the table and squeeze her hand, really quickly. "Puh-lease do not worry about it. It's really not a big deal. You're a good friend." I unwrap the cookie, break a big piece off, and pop it in my mouth. "This was so nice of you. Thank you. D'you want some?"

But Erin doesn't brighten immediately the way I'd hoped she would.

Still frowning, she grabs a strand of long hair and twists it between her fingers. "I know it's not really your style to spill every little thing you're thinking and feeling like I do. I get that you're kind of a private person, but . . . I just wanted to say that I'm here, okay?"

She looks at me, expectant. She just sits there and waits, and I realize I'm going to have to give her *something.*

I shift to the right, gazing uncomfortably out the wall of windows behind our table. I think back to Friday night, sitting beside Alex, telling him about my brother. His response had been surprising, encouraging even.

Where was the harm in telling one more person?

Except . . .

I chew on my lower lip and consider some more.

Except . . . there is a lens through which we view every single other person in this world. With every piece of information we gain about them, the lens is adjusted, ever so slightly, blurring . . . coloring . . . *changing* how we see them.

Erin's perception of me has never been affected by the knowledge of Phillip's existence and I don't want that to change.

And Erin is so incredibly image conscious, analyzing every little thing anyone ever says about her. She'd heard how the kids at the party were talking about Phillip. If she knew he was my brother . . .

I clam back up, imperceptibly.

I turn my clear, steady gaze back toward Erin. "Just some minor family drama." I pause before adding, "With my mom."

Mom drama is part and parcel to being a teenage girl. It's as good an explanation as any.

But Erin is not easily pacified and shakes her head. "I don't understand, though. We were all having a really good time on Friday night. You were in a good mood—at dinner, at the game, even, like, five minutes before you took off and disappeared. What changed so quickly? Did you get a phone call or something? Did something happen?"

I grit my teeth, guarding myself against her barrage of insistent questions. "Nothing like that. Just a delayed reaction to something. I'm sure drinking didn't help. Made me over-emotional."

Erin still looks confused, determined, and maybe even a little irritated. "But you still haven't said what happened," she persists.

I try to inhale a deep breath through my clenched teeth. Mentally, I count to ten, so my voice is calm when I respond. "Erin." I smile pleasantly at her and shrug apologetically. "What you said before? Is probably true. When it comes to family drama, I'm sort of a private person and I . . . I just don't want to get into it."

She stares at me for a long minute, trying to absorb such a foreign concept. Erin would willingly detail her long litany of daily crises with a stranger on the street, so she has no way of making sense of my tendency to keep my woes bottled up. But eventually, she concedes the battle. "Okay, well . . ." She shrugs. "I offered, right?"

"Right. And I appreciate it."

Convinced it's the end of our uncomfortable discussion, I flip open my workbook to the review problems for lesson five and finally get to work. I've only finished one equation when Erin interrupts me.

"Oh, hey, don't forget, I have to give my book-review presentation in English tomorrow. Is it still okay if I borrow that purple skirt of yours? The one from J.Crew? I want to look nice."

"You always look nice, Erin. But, yeah, that's totally fine. You can borrow it."

"Cool. Can I follow you home after practice? Pick it up?"

I shake my head instinctively. "Ugh, no, that's probably not the greatest timing." I utter the same excuse I've given about a hundred times. "My mom's working third shift at the hospital tonight, and if someone new comes over, our dog goes nutso, and it'll wake her up, and I try really hard not to do that."

I feel a sick shame twisting in my stomach as I lie to my friend, and try to tell myself there's some semblance of truth in what I just told her. Once upon a time my mom *did* work third shift at the hospital, but she hasn't worked as a nurse in years. She couldn't handle the rotating schedule and still make herself available every time she got a phone call from Phillip's school that he needed to be picked up and taken home, when he was really out of control. But once, my story could have been true.

"I'll make sure I get here really early tomorrow," I promise. "So you have plenty of time to change."

"But I wanted to make sure it fits. And that it looks right with my boots. I don't have to come in tonight," she assures me. "I could just wait in the driveway if you don't mind running in to get it."

"I'm a size four, you're a size four. You're only an inch taller than I am. I'm sure it'll fit. I'll just bring it in tomorrow."

I return my attention to problem number two, trying to focus. Before I've even read it, I hear a shuddery, choked sound from across the table. My head jerks up in surprise and my eyes widen as I assess the tears filling Erin's eyes.

"What's wrong?" I ask, genuinely shocked. I get that Erin's worrying when it comes to outfit planning is a big deal, but this is excessive, even for her. "If it's that big a deal, you can pick up the skirt tonight."

"That's not what I'm upset about," she answers, voice

quivering with tears. She bats at her eyes with the back of her hand, and meets my eyes. "I mean . . . Jordyn . . . do you even *want* to be friends with me?"

"What?"

She shrugs and shakes her head. "I don't know. I mean, we're supposed to be friends, but you have no interest in talking to me when you're upset, and I end up feeling like I'm making you feel *worse* rather than better when I bother to ask you anything. And then I just want to stop over for five minutes and it seems like it's the biggest bother in the world. God. Some days I feel like I'm pestering you more than anything else."

I close my eyes against the stirring of the headache pressing against my temples. If I'd had any idea our conversation was going to take this turn, I definitely would have agreed to let her come over to pick up the damn skirt.

I open my eyes and look at my friend. "Please don't feel that way," I beg her. "I'm sorry I'm a crappy friend sometimes, but don't take it personally."

"You're not a crappy friend. It's just like . . . when I try to be a good friend to you, sometimes it feels like you don't even want that. Like you don't want anyone around you. And sometimes it's just really hard *not* to take it personally."

I stare at her helplessly. "That's just me," I eventually mumble. "And all I can do is promise you that it has nothing to do with you. You're my closest friend at Valley Forge. I can't imagine being here without having you as a friend."

This is true, and I hate hurting her.

Erin smiles shakily. "You sure?"

"I'm sure." I wave my hand dismissively. "I'm a weirdo sometimes, I know. Don't read too much into the things I say or do."

She wipes at her eyes a final time and pulls out a pressed powder compact to check her makeup. "Alright. I'll try. Sorry for pushing you."

"Nothing to be sorry about. I know you're just trying to be a good friend."

We finally shift our focus to homework, but my concentration has been destroyed. I'm way more upset than I'm letting on about how I've made Erin feel. I try to tell myself that it's not all my fault and that Erin's insecurities get the better of her all the time. I tell myself that I can make this up to her. I'll surprise her and drive the skirt over to her house tonight, and I'll take some accessories along with it, too. I tell myself this will blow over.

But at heart, I understand it's my behavior more than anything else that caused Erin's tears, and it's a crummy realization to carry around for the rest of the day. A personal skirt delivery isn't going to fix anything, not in the long run. It's not going to change anything. It's not going to turn our friendship into a two-way street.

Erin and I walk together toward the junior hallway for our fifth-period classes, passing the converted Home Ec/Autistic Support classroom on our way. The door is closed, but I can see, and hear, Phillip behind it. His face is practically pressed against the glass and he is shrieking about something. Or everything. Or nothing at all. Anne is saying all the right things to encourage him to return to his seat, but as always, he is oblivious.

Phillip is so damn oblivious to the damage he causes. It's

Phillip's world and he can't see beyond it to how *his* world sometimes really messes up other people's worlds.

Neither my foul mood nor my headache has subsided by the time I get home after practice. In fact, my head is pounding harder than ever, because persistent rain showers moved practice indoors. It was way too loud in the gym, our coach's yells echoing off the bleachers and her whistle louder and shriller than ever.

I'm still preoccupied with worries about my conversation with Erin. I really don't want to lose her as a friend, and I hate the idea that she might eventually start pulling away from me if I don't start behaving the way a so-called normal friend is expected to.

Things with Alex were weird during independent study, too. I can't say he did or said anything differently than he always does, but something was definitely off between us. It left me wondering if Leighton had already talked to him about the way things needed to change. I couldn't be myself with him, either. My instincts told me Leighton's claim that he'd referred to me as a sister was a lie, but I couldn't fully eradicate the idea that it could be true.

What if he really does see me like a sister? What if his parting words at the bonfire were nothing special?

What if I'm completely delusional about any lingering anything between us?

I am drained and confused, my head spinning in twenty different directions on the drive home.

When I walk into the kitchen, it's obvious that my mom is

in a much better mood than I am. She is seated at the center island, literally beaming at her iPad.

"What's going on?" I mumble tiredly.

Her smile widens further. "I just got the most exciting phone call!"

I drop my stuff and wait for her to elaborate. Unless her news involves Phillip's immediate transfer to a different school, I doubt I'll share her enthusiasm.

"You know how Terry Roth is involved with the Happiness Circuit?"

I nod. Terry Roth, Phillip's behavior specialist, the one I'd ignored at school, works with the charity in her free time.

The name of the charity is pretty self-explanatory. The organization's basic mission is to spread some cheer among kids who are sick or just facing unfortunate circumstances. Volunteers help collect and deliver toys, games, DVDs, even computers. They get kids into celebrity meet-and-greets, concerts, sporting events, and theme parks. Sometimes they just go on junk-food runs or organize Nerf water-gun wars for kids stuck in the local children's hospitals.

"Well," my mom continues, tapping the screen of her iPad, "every year in November, they sponsor the Sparkle Ball in Philadelphia."

I hover over her shoulder, reading the description of the event on the screen. It is, apparently, "a black-tie celebration and fundraising gala akin to a Hollywood event." Children battling chronic illnesses or other life-altering conditions are to be recognized for their courage and resilience; for one night, they are treated like movie stars. The evening includes a fancy dinner, live music and dancing, silent auctions and raffles, and games for the kids in one of the ballrooms at the downtown Four Seasons.

"It's a night for these brave children to shine!" the Web site boasts.

"Terry nominated Phillip as an attendee," my mom explains. "She submitted his math PSAT scores from when he took them last year."

All college-bound students are required to take the standardized math and language test in eleventh grade, but statewide, students can opt to take a practice version of the test as eighth graders. Students who perform particularly well are honored with certificates of achievement and listed in "who's who" booklets mailed out to parents willing to shell out twenty-five dollars to receive a copy.

Phillip was more than happy to sit for two hours, wearing his headphones, and complete math problems in an empty, silent room. Given the accommodations he needed, he nailed the test. His score was higher than mine from my eighth-grade testing session.

"Terry just called to tell me Phillip was picked to receive an invitation!" My mom practically bounces on the stool. "And even more exciting? This is the first time the organization is recognizing students with autism for overcoming life challenges. Can you believe it, the *first* time, like kids haven't been struggling with this diagnosis for years and years? Anyway, there's Phillip, and a little girl they selected as well."

My mom grabs my arm and shakes it. "Isn't this exciting?!" Terry says the event's a really big deal. A lot of people get limos and the families get to walk a red carpet and everything. There's

TV coverage. We'll all get dressed up, and you can get a new dress, and—"

The hammer in my head turns into a power drill.

Is she out of her damn mind?

"Umm . . . I'm not going." I interrupt her excited monologue in a heavy, flat voice.

She stares back at me, mouth open slightly, surprised. I have extinguished her joy at once, like a damper to a candle.

"Have you lost your mind?" I ask. "Phillip would hate that. He would *hate* it. Everything about it. I mean, television coverage? Really, Mom?"

My mom stares down at the countertop. She powers off the iPad, and spreads her hands flat on the island on either side of it. "He should get to hear people clap for him, Jordyn," she says quietly. "Just once."

I laugh bitterly. "Even if people clapping for him is something that he'd *hate*?"

My mom still refuses to meet my eyes. She stares at the dark, blank screen. I bet she is wishing I never came home, that she was still reading about the ball and imagining a perfect night.

Maybe I should be merciful, but I can't seem to stop dousing her with reality. "It's not like Phillip is going to change, Mom. It's not like he's going to just snap out of it." I shake my head at the ridiculousness of the Sparkle Ball. "It's not like one day he's going to look back and be *glad* you forced him to go. You realize that, right?"

"It doesn't matter if he has a hard time," she insists stubbornly. "He won't stand out there. All the kids will have needs.

Only people who truly want to be there will be there. It won't be other people being forced to deal with him."

I am tired and frustrated with everything. In the moment, I am mean-spirited.

I fold my arms across my chest and take a step back. "Well, don't count me in as one of those people. I'm not going."

My mom turns to assess me head-on. She stares at me a long time, as if I'm a stranger, a person she does not recognize standing in her kitchen. "What's going on with you today?"

Somehow, her voice is still kind.

Mine is still not.

I look her square in the eye. "I just wish you'd be honest about all of this. This night isn't for Phillip at all. This night is for you. It's selfish."

She pales right before me. Her throat constricts. "Do you need to be so cutting?" she asks, her voice quiet and broken.

"I'm just calling a spade a spade." I walk past her, calling over my shoulder, "I have to drop something off at Erin's. I'll be back in a while."

My mom doesn't try to stop me and I don't really blame her.

I can feel the acid in the pit of my stomach and taste it in my mouth when I'm being a bitch, and I don't really like the way it feels any more than I'm sure she does.

But I'm not deluded enough to get excited about this dance. I think she's straight-up crazy for thinking it's a good idea, and I don't understand why she'd want to subject *any* of us to such a fiasco. It would be great to escape to a world where Phillip can be treated like a movie star, and act like one, for a single night. I get it.

I stomp up the stairs and yank the purple skirt from my closet.

But welcome back to reality, Mom. There's no such thing as a night off from autism. Not for Phillip. Not for me. And not for you.

Before I leave my room, I flip the cover back on my agenda and draw an angry X through the day. Even though it's almost halfway over at this point, today, surviving another day brings little satisfaction.

Chapter Eight

On Saturday morning, I'm set to head out to Alex's workday at the playground. I'm dressed for warmth and ready to get down to serious business in beat-up jeans, an ancient Hollister hoodie, and a knit hat. Before leaving my room, I make sure to grab the bag of special supplies I ordered online after Alex gave me my assignment last week.

As I walk down the hallway to the stairs, I hear my mom rustling around in our fourth bedroom, which is still serving as an office–slash–craft room–slash–storage space after the move. I hesitate outside. It would be much easier to keep walking, but really, I should tell her where I'm going. I take a deep breath and enter the room.

"I'm heading out now. I'm going to help Alex with his project."

My mother, situated on the floor working on one project or another, doesn't bother to lift her head. "Okay." Her single-word response is clipped and brisk.

She's been pretty icy toward me since our exchange on Monday night, and I know she's well within her right to be acting like this. I was mean and hurtful. Since then, I've thought about apologizing a bunch of times, but I just haven't. Our fight feels too recent and raw, and I can't force the words out of my mouth.

We are both pretending nothing happened, while avoiding each other at the same time. My father is oblivious. I can tell she hasn't told him about the incident or my behavior, which somehow makes me feel *worse*.

I wring my hands, thinking I'm really tired of the tension between us.

"I'm really sorry for what I said," I blurt out.

She waits a minute before turning toward me and lifting her eyes to mine. Her expression is flat. "Are you?"

"What do you mean?"

"Are you really sorry? For what? For saying what you said out loud?" She shakes her head and returns her gaze to the floor. "It's not like it's something you don't believe or didn't mean," she murmurs.

Her blunt honesty catches me off guard. It's not something I'm used to from her. I stand in the doorway, more tongue-tied than ever. The truth is, she's right, and I can't deny the thoughts and feelings I'd thrown in her face. But that doesn't mean I don't feel bad.

"I'm sorry for how I said it. I'm sorry for hurting your feelings and ruining your day."

It's the best I can offer.

She studies me for a while, assessing my intent. I guess I pass her test, because her face clears and she reaches up from the floor to squeeze my hand. "Thanks for that," she says simply. "You're forgiven."

A great sense of relief overtakes me, and my shoulders relax. It has felt like a very long week, with the way we've been tiptoeing around each other.

Eager to move past the ugliness between us, I look down at her project, wanting to change the subject. She's sitting on the carpet with a gigantic pink box in front of her. It's the size and length of the kind of box you'd use to store a wedding dress or something, wrapped in pretty paper that has started to yellow.

I step into the room and examine the box's contents, immediately recognizing mementos from my many childhood successes: blue and red ribbons from summertime swim meets, art projects that won awards in the annual school show, goldenrod report cards with lines of straight As and glowing teacher comments, small trophies from gymnastics and ballet—both of which I'd given up on years ago—random certificates of achievement, and newspaper clippings from the "Kids' Corner" where my fourth-grade poetry attempts were published. The box is meticulously organized, with smaller boxes and labeled file folders inside, cataloging my accomplishments in a year-by-year system.

"What are you doing?" I ask.

She holds up a newspaper clipping. "I'm adding the newspaper article about this year's team," she answers, referring to the write-up on the varsity field hockey squad that Leighton had probably commissioned. "There are a few other things I haven't filed yet, like your report card from the end of last year."

"You save *everything*?" I pick up a misshapen clay pot and roll my eyes. "I mean, is this really worthy of saving for posterity?"

"I'm your mother." She smiles wanly. "I think everything you do is beautiful, and special, and wonderful. It's hard to think about throwing anything away, like it's not important. Everything you do is important to me."

Truly, my little clay pot does not deserve this kind of admiration. Parents are funny creatures.

My mom takes a deep breath and hesitates, like she's scared of what she has to say next.

"I don't want to start another fight with you," she begins slowly, "but I want to show you something."

She gets up, rummages around in the closet, and pulls out a box that's identical to my pink one, but wrapped in yellowing blue paper. Structurally, it is more sound—it does not sag in the middle and its corners are intact. My mom carries it easily, like it's feather light. "This is Phillip's box. Nanny gave me yours, and she gave me one for him, too, when he was born. They were meant to be keepsake boxes."

My mom sets it on the floor beside mine and opens it. Its contents are stark in comparison, and no yearly file folders are required to keep them organized. There are a few school pictures from years he managed to smile, a kind note from a teacher Phillip developed a really great relationship with, his score printout from the math PSATs. My box is full and overflowing—beside it, his box looks like a joke.

From beneath my sophomore year report card and the recent field hockey newspaper article, my mom pulls a printout of the e-mail from Terry about the Happiness Circuit nomination and the invitation to the Sparkle Ball.

"What I just said to you, Jordyn? How as your mom, I see

everything you do as beautiful, and special, and wonderful?" She runs the palm of her hand over one of Phillip's pictures. "I feel the same exact way about your brother, alright? Accomplishments are measured on a much smaller scale, and I have to find different things beautiful—the way he examines a fallen leaf during autumn, those brief moments when he checks into this planet to ask me a question about how something works, his silly laughter, his smiles . . . but I feel the exact same way."

She shakes her head, and her voice tightens. "It's easy for me. But the rest of the world doesn't recognize Phillip the way the rest of the world recognizes you." She points toward my box. "Look at all these things, how many times I've gotten to sit in an audience and have other people acknowledge just how awesome my kid is." My mom stares into my eyes, and I wish I could ignore the glassy cast to hers. "You think it's selfish, but it's not. It's this feeling like the love and joy you find in your child can't possibly be contained in your heart alone, this feeling like the world should celebrate your child, too. Every child should be celebrated that way, at least once." Her throat convulses and her voice drops to a whisper. "It comes with being a parent, and I don't think I was being selfish for wanting that, just once, for Phillip."

"Mom—"

She waves her hand in protest and wipes at her eyes. Eventually, she forces a laugh. "I know it's a pipe dream, all of it—the idea that I'd be able to coax him into a tux, the idea that he'd *actually* walk down that red carpet, the idea that he'd realize what the night is for and enjoy any part of it. But I want that for him, anyway."

She stops trying to laugh the pain away and she looks sadder than I've seen her look in a long while. "I'm never going to get what I want, but still . . . I can't seem to stop wanting people to fill his box the way people have filled yours."

I hover above her, silent. I guess in my mother's eyes, Phillip and I are more alike than different.

I stare down at his image, smiling in the school picture. Phillip reduces everything, everyone, to objects and it's easy to do the same to him. To view him as a highly irritable robot, whose programming is rife with bugs and flaws, creating disconnects every time he tries to interact with humans. Looking at this picture, you'd never know. He's just as human as I am, and it's *not* right that his box is empty, I decide.

But we can't change the world, and we sure as hell can't change Phillip's world, so what she wants, yeah, it seems like a pipe dream. And I hate the idea of her having to face reality and the idea of other people, Phillip included, letting her down. That's really what I'd been trying to say to her the other night, but my own feelings got in the way.

"I just don't want you to be disappointed if the night doesn't turn out the way you want it to."

My mom turns toward me a final time and squares her shoulders. "If I worried about disappointment when it comes to Phillip, he'd never be where he is today, Jordyn. I can hardly let the fear of my expectations falling short, the idea of people letting me down, dictate how we live around here."

Something catches within me.

Her words poke at a truth buried within me, reminding me of ways in which I am weak.

I hurriedly push my sleeve up and glance at my watch. "Well. I'm going to be really late soon. I should get going."

"Thanks for stopping to chat." She offers a small smile in parting.

I nod once and scurry toward the front door, away from the discomfort our conversation has provoked.

After getting caught up talking to my mom, I'm running late to meet the work crew at the playground. But I need a few minutes to clear my head, so I stop and pick up a bagel and coffee at the Einstein Bros I pass on my way. As an afterthought, I add a cinnamon raisin bagel, Alex's favorite, to my order. Knowing him, he's probably been at the playground site since the crack of dawn.

When I pull up to the park, the dirt lot is full of cars, and in the distance, I see groups of people already hard at work. I'm not surprised that Alex has gotten a good turnout of friends from school and members of the community. As I approach the crowd and find Leighton manning the snack table for volunteers, I'm glad I can blend in as one friend of many.

Even so, I stash the Einstein Bros bag in my purse as I near the group. She's beat me to the punch, anyway. The table is covered with artfully arranged trays of fruit and dip, bagels and gourmet cream cheese, and danishes and doughnut holes. There are plastic carafes of fruit juice and thermoses of coffee.

I guess manning the snack table is Leighton's only task, because she doesn't seem very motivated to move beyond it. She's relaxing in a folding chair with her feet up, sipping from a cup of coffee and talking to Dana and Jamie like today is a social gathering more than anything else. It doesn't escape my attention that she's taped a flyer advertising the hockey team's upcoming spaghetti dinner fund-raiser for new equipment to the front of the table. There is a cash box and a pile of tickets in front of her.

Even though I'd love to avoid them entirely, I force myself to say hi.

"Jordyn's here. Shocking," Dana quips.

Leighton is all business as she points toward the box. "We're multitasking today. Did you buy tickets for your family yet? The team should really have one hundred percent attendance."

I'm aware of her 100 percent goal, but, no, I have most certainly *not* bought tickets for my family yet.

I open my purse and pull out some money, thinking maybe my mom won't mind going by herself, since I'll be working the event.

I hand Leighton a twenty-dollar bill. "My dad's tied up that night, but I think my mom can come. Just one ticket's fine." Tickets are only ten dollars, but I wave the change aside. "Keep the change, as a donation. I'm sure my parents won't mind."

Hopefully, this will appease her.

She nods her approval, and as she hands me one ticket, I notice Alex approaching. His face is serious and focused, but he looks as appealing as ever in cargo pants, a gray hoodie, and a navy knit hat that makes his beautiful brown eyes stand out even more than normal. His cheeks are flushed from exertion and the cold.

"Hi, Jordyn. Thanks again for making it out today. Was keeping an eye out for you."

It's an innocent enough comment, but internally I cringe, thinking how the words will sound to Leighton and crew.

"Sorry I'm running so late," I spit out in a rush, taking a step away from him. "I got caught up talking to my mom, and—"

Leighton interrupts me. "We're right on top of things at our post, Alex," she informs him cheerily. She tightens her scarf around her neck. "Making sure workers stay fed and warm and happy. Everyone'll be more productive that way."

Alex's expression becomes colored with some low-burning frustration, and he just smiles tightly at her in response.

Leighton doesn't seem to notice though, and continues on. "And like I just told your buddy Jordyn, I'm multitasking. Like a boss. I already sold more than twenty tickets to the spaghetti dinner, and it's only ten thirty."

I think his annoyance is obvious now, in the set of his jaw and darkness of his eyes, but she still doesn't seem to get it.

"I'm gonna get Jordyn started," he says tersely, grabbing my elbow and steering me away from the table. I try to picture what Leighton's face must look like, but I sure as hell don't want to turn around to see. He is *not* helping me out here.

I don't relax until we round the corner of the bathrooms and three pairs of eyes are no longer on my back.

Alex's mood seems to lift as well and his smile turns genuine. "So . . . all set for latrine duty?"

"Yeah. I just wish you'd stop calling it that."

"Again, if you'd rather, I can get you a hammer." He points toward a group of guys from school who are squinting at a diagram as they attempt to put together a complicated-looking see-saw apparatus.

"I'll stick with latrines. As long as I just have to paint."

Alex nods toward the entrance. "Come on, then, I'll show you. Get ready to Seussify the place."

I giggle and smile as I follow his lead.

Alex, in conjunction with the charity organization sponsoring the playground development, had decided on a whimsical, colorful design scheme based on popular Dr. Seuss books and characters. The plans include red-and-white-striped poles, à la the Cat in the Hat, and the main path leading to the playground is going to be painted in pastel-colored stripes like the road in *Oh, the Places You'll Go!* A local artist has been commissioned to craft a large, sweeping banner over the entrance, one that will bear the quote, "Today you are you, that is truer than true. There is no one alive who is youer than you!"

I adore the theme and think it's perfect for what Alex is trying to accomplish by getting this playground built.

He leads me into the small stucco bathroom building, the interior of which has been slated to receive a dousing of orange, blue, and white, to represent the color scheme from *Horton Hears a Who!*, the book about the compassionate elephant who looks out for those smaller than he. The main walls have already been given a base coat, but I'll be responsible for working on the wooden stall frames and doors, along with the wooden frames surrounding the mirrors. It's not a terrible job. There are no confusing diagrams involved, at least.

Alex goes over the basics with me, and I nod. "No problem.

I helped paint the sets for a few plays at my old school. This'll be easy-peasy."

Alex quirks an eyebrow and his dimple appears. "Easy-peasy?"

"Yes, easy-peasy."

He laughs, and I am happy to see him brighten again, even at my silly terminology. "Easy-peasy. If you say so. Alright, well, Dan and Mitch are over working on the boys' bathroom side, but if you want some help, I can pull Dana or Jamie away from Leighton." He doesn't bother to stifle an eye roll. "I don't really think you need three people to hand out bagels, but . . ."

"I'll be fine," I say quickly, because I don't want to spend the day trapped inside a small bathroom with either one of them. Plus, I have my secret supply stash that I don't want to explain to them. "I'll yell if I fall into a paint vat, or a toilet, or something."

Alex chuckles one more time before his voice turns serious. "Okay. And thanks again, Michaelson. I really appreciate it."

"Happy to help," I answer.

"What are you working on?" I ask, as he turns to leave. "Just supervising? Shouldn't you have a hard hat or something?"

My favorite grin lights up his face, causing the dimple to re-appear. "I don't, but you're right, I should. That would be amazing." He shakes his head. "No, actually, I'm working on one of the wheelchair ramps." He shrugs. "I helped install a couple at home, so actually I *am* sort of the crew chief. Not sure anyone else knows what they're doing." Alex suddenly looks concerned. "In fact, yeah, I better get back out there. See ya later, M.J."

"See ya later."

He turns to leave, I take a second to watch him go, and then I get to work.

I'm pretty adept with paintbrushes and rollers, from my work on the play sets I told Alex about and because I've painted my bedroom several times over the year. I can work with precision around the blue tape strips, and I know how to edge like a pro. It's a bit more complicated when it comes to painting the stall doors because I have to stand on a step stool to reach their tops, but there are only three of them to worry about.

I take a break around lunchtime, when Alex has a bunch of pizzas delivered. I want to make sure to check in with him, rather than having him check in on me later, when I plan to work on the surprise part of my project. I don't get to talk privately to Alex, though, because Leighton is too busy drawing him into some very public recognition.

When everyone has gathered around a few rickety picnic tables, balancing slices of pepperoni and mushroom on flimsy paper plates, Leighton claps her hands loudly and bellows for everyone's attention.

"Before we all get back to work . . . ," she starts.

I consider how her definition of work differs from mine. Sitting behind a table peddling tickets and talking to friends is a far cry from how most of us spent the morning.

". . . I just wanted to take a minute for everyone to acknowledge how hard Alex has been working to make this project spectacular."

She stands behind the table, beaming, pointing in his direction and winking before leading everyone in a big round of applause. "This is a huge deal and he's totally going to turn it into a success. I mean, can we just take a minute to acknowledge how awesome this guy is?"

Everyone joins her in applauding and she throws in some whooping on top of the cheers.

I study her as I halfheartedly join the cheering. Her enthusiasm and praise of her boyfriend sure seem genuine. Nothing she says is untrue, and I don't think Alex would've hated the recognition if we were just among friends.

But with adults from the community and fund contributors standing about, it's wrong to focus the admiration on a single person when so many are involved in the project's completion. It's just all so very Leighton, but it isn't Alex at all. I shift my attention to his face, and I can tell he's less than thrilled about the attention being focused on him instead of the project overall.

Leighton leaves right after lunch. I hear her ask Alex, "I mean, snack time is over, right? Do you mind if we take off? I have some things to take care of, and I should really drop the cash box back at school."

It does not cross her mind that maybe she could help elsewhere, that no one else is gearing up to leave.

Alex just nods. He steps forward to plant a quick kiss on her lips. But he doesn't reach out to touch her, and his eyes are even farther away than his body.

The first day of school, I had a pretty emotional reaction to seeing them together. Jealous. There, I said it. I felt jealous.

But in this moment, I don't. I feel sad for my friend, whose girlfriend seems so entirely oblivious to how his mind and heart work. It must be a pretty lonely feeling for him.

I get back to work as everyone else does. I'm happy to find

that the paint has dried enough for me to begin phase two of my project.

When Alex told me about the theme for the bathroom, I looked around online and discovered these stencils and decals to create murals in kids' rooms and doctors' offices. I was so excited when I found the Horton characters in the online catalogue that I ordered several.

Now I work to arrange them carefully on the stall doors so it appears that the characters are peeking out from the edges of the doors. I plaster a second stencil at wheelchair height on the main wall behind the sink. I take my time painting the letters until Horton's mantra is complete: "A person's a person, no matter how small."

It's hard work, requiring precision and focus, and it consumes me. Eventually, I notice the sun beginning to set behind the hills through the one small window in the bathroom, but I refuse to stop until I'm finished. I don't want Alex to see anything less than a finished project. I am thirsty, I have to pee, and my back is stiff from bending over to paint the lower sections of the mural. But eventually, I paint the last tuft of hair on Horton's head and stand up to examine my work.

There is Horton, smiling out from the corner of one door, with a little Who from Whoville balanced precariously on his head. The Wickersham monkey brothers swing from the top of the second stall. There is the Mama Kangaroo, with her baby in her pouch, staring haughtily at a whole village of little Whos on the last door in the room.

A huge smile spreads over my face. The murals look even better than I imagined. They look awesome.

I'm still standing with my back against the wall, admiring my work, when I hear the door open. Alex walks in. "Christ, M.J., you're still here? I figured you'd left by now and I just missed—"

He stops dead in his tracks. His eyes widen, and his mouth actually falls open. He looks at me in amazement, looks back at the doors, and then back at me. "Are you kidding me? What is this?"

I lower my gaze and shrug dismissively. "It's the Horton bathroom, obviously," I say, gesturing toward the orange paint on the walls.

"Yes, but . . . what's the rest of it?"

I swallow hard and manage to meet his eye. "That's my contribution."

Alex comes over and stands beside me, so close that our sleeves are touching. He adopts my position, arms folded across his chest, as he stares at the paintings some more.

"Jordyn, this looks awesome. Did you actually *paint* these?"

"Oh, I had stencils. They're really easy to use. Trust me, I'm not that artistic."

"Where'd you get this stuff?"

"Online. You can find anything online."

"I'll reimburse you," he assures me quickly.

"Nope. Like I said, it's my contribution, and they weren't expensive."

I take a deep breath and look over at him, which isn't easy at all, considering how close he is. As soon as my eyes meet his, I feel like talking is no longer a skill that comes easily. "I, uh, hope you don't mind that I didn't ask first. I wanted to surprise you. Figured I could always paint over it, if you hated it."

Alex's eyes widen in protest. "Hate it? I love it!"

He stares at me for another minute, the look in his eyes a confusing combination of gratitude, warmth, and . . . sadness? He allows the back of his hand to tap against the back of mine. "I love that you wanted to do this," he whispers.

"Well, you're making everything around here special," I reply. I try to laugh, but it gets stuck in my throat. I can hardly breathe, with him looking at me like that. "You know. The 'latrines' should be special, too."

Alex shakes his head, at a loss. "I've said thank you a lot today, I've said it to a lot of people. I have no idea how to say thank you for this."

"You don't have to."

"Yes, I do." He turns so he is facing me now. I turn toward him. We are practically touching and I can feel the soft, heavy fabric of his sweatshirt against mine. I smell wood shavings and cologne. I feel warmth.

His right palm lands on the space above his heart. He taps it, twice. "Thank you," he whispers. "Seriously, Jordyn."

He looks at me, I look at him.

I taste desire.

I only ever allow myself to see my friend Alex anymore, but in this moment, he's gone. I stare at the boy who stole my heart last summer and he's looking right back at me. My heart seizes up, because I've really, really missed him.

I thought he was gone forever, but maybe . . .

I hear his sharp intake of breath. I remember it instantly, remember how I heard it in the darkness right before he kissed me. He quickly licks his lips.

But this time he does not close the distance between us. Instead, he steps back, creating distance all over again. He clenches his fists at his sides as I watch a frustrated sadness consume his expression. Alex looks past me, gazing through the small window. The sun is setting and the light in the small room is fading fast. I'm left feeling particularly chilled.

Alex takes off his hat, runs his hand back and forth over his matted hair, and coughs. "It's getting dark," he mumbles. "They don't have the lights up and running yet, so I should really go pack up the truck."

I nod, bending over to begin picking up the materials I've left strewn about, finding it impossible to look at him. It will hurt, because I know the person I just saw a glimpse of has disappeared anew.

Exhausted, I slowly gather decal backings, rinse brushes, and stash the rollers and empty cans into large orange buckets. I drag them outside, stumbling through the darkness toward Alex, who is packing tools and supplies into the back of his uncle's pickup truck.

Outside, I can breathe again. I plaster a smile on my face and slip back into my role: Jordyn Michaelson, Supportive Friend. Nothing More.

"You must be beat," I say brightly. "Gonna go home and crash?"

But he doesn't look at me and his voice is still constricted. "For a while. Then I have to go out with Leighton."

Have to?

It's an interesting choice of words, so I wait for him to continue.

He exhales a sigh of frustration through his nose and slams the panel on the back of the truck bed. He turns and leans against it, crossing his arms over his chest, and glowers into the darkness.

"Summer was fun, when we had some space and it was just this new thing, but being back at school . . ." He shakes his head and lets a thin wisp of air escape between his lips. "Sometimes it's like I'm just here for decoration," he muses gloomily. He glances at me, just for a second, before looking into the distance again. "She somehow managed to make today about her, didn't she? Or at least . . . she managed to make today the way *she* thought it should go. It's always like everything is hers."

I would love to agree with him because what he's said is so very true. But it wouldn't be very Supportive Friend of me to do so.

I shake my head mildly. "Well. I'm sure she didn't have bad intentions, at any rate."

"Yeah, maybe." He puffs up his cheeks and exhales mightily. "But I don't know. . . ."

He fumbles for his keys in his pocket and starts to turn away, like he's getting ready to leave. But before he even takes a single step, he turns back, face resolute, eyes determined. "No. I do know, actually." He pauses for only a second before spitting it out. "I'm not in love with her. I *do* know that."

I am stunned into silence, because it's an admission I've never expected to hear. I look back at him, at a loss, trying to remind myself that nothing he's just said really has anything to do with me, anyway.

Then Alex obliterates my ability to separate myself from it.

"I'm not in love with her . . . ," he repeats, pulling a tissue from his jeans pocket and running it over my left cheek. When he pulls it away, I see a streak of orange paint. He crumbles the tissue in his fist with unnecessary force. ". . . and sometimes being reminded of that really freakin' sucks."

My breath catches in my throat at the harshness in his words, the repressed emotion underlying them. My heart picks up, pounding loud and insistent against my chest. I look up at him, thankful for the cloak of darkness that gives me half a chance of standing this ground.

Alex stares right back at me. "Listen, Jordyn . . . ," he begins.

He doesn't get a chance to say anything else.

Dan, Mitch, and Jason appear over the crest of the small hill to our left. They are sweaty and laughing, and Mitch has a basketball cradled in the crook of his right arm. They must've squeezed in a quick game on the courts after calling it quits on the playground.

Alex had been reaching toward me. His hand still hovers awkwardly near mine.

They must all notice. Jason, who is dating Dana, Leighton's best friend, surely must notice.

I step away from Alex and turn toward them. I force myself to wave heartily and adopt my cheeriest voice. "Have a good night, guys!" I call loudly. I turn back toward Alex, voice still loud and artificial. "You, too, Alex!"

I jog toward my car, not bothering to wait for a response from him, trying to erase from my memory the disappointed look I've left on his face in my wake.

Chapter Nine

There are twenty-four days left after today in my countdown to when everything starts to unravel. I guess I'm thankful I'm not there when the pivotal thread is first tugged.

I leave school early for a dentist's appointment. The chaotic office is running on time for once, and I get back home a half hour earlier than I'd expected to when I told Coach Marks I'd be missing practice.

The lazy thing to do, the thing I *want* to do, is stay at home and relish an unexpected afternoon off. Not for the sake of being productive and getting my homework done or anything. I have visions of sour cream and onion Pringles and watching *Awkward* reruns on MTV2 before Phillip shows up and reclaims the television.

I open the front door and sigh as I stare at my gym bag hanging in the mudroom. Forget the chips and bad TV. The right thing to do is get changed as quickly as possible and head back to school in time for practice. If I hurry, I'll only miss opening stretches. We do have a game tomorrow.

But before I can dash upstairs, my attention is drawn into the kitchen. I walk toward the back of the house, hovering behind the doorframe, eavesdropping on my mom's phone conversation.

Her back is to me and her shoulders are hunched, but I can tell she's tiredly rubbing her forehead. It's obvious she's upset, but her voice is defeated, unsurprised. "Right, right . . . mmm-hmm . . . I understand."

She shoves carelessly at the tendrils that have escaped her low ponytail. "And no other ideas as to what led to this? It was just the iPad situation that stood out today?"

Hidden in the doorway, I stiffen. It isn't hard to guess what, or who, had caused her insta-migraine.

My mom listens for another minute, her hand still on her forehead. She clears her throat. "As always, I'm so terribly sorry. I'm sorry this isn't easier for all of you there."

My fingers tighten around the doorframe and I roll my eyes. We hadn't decided to send Phillip back to school—what is she apologizing for?

"And as I'm sure Mrs. Akers and Anne saw in his daily log today, his medication was tweaked last week, but we started the dosage adjustment over the weekend so that we could keep an eye on him. We didn't notice anything different on Saturday or Sunday, so I'm not sure if that could've had something to do with his heightened agitation or not." She braces herself on the island and shakes her head back and forth. "Anyway. Where is he now?"

Another moment passes and then she is nodding her head

again. "No, certainly, I understand. That's okay. I can come pick him up." She grabs the car keys off the hook near the phone receiver. "I'm walking out the door as we speak."

My mom hangs up the phone without bothering to say goodbye. I don't anticipate how quickly she moves, grabbing her down vest and purse and spinning in my direction within seconds. She is distracted and nearly crashes into me. A muffled gasp escapes her, and her hand flies to her chest. "Jordyn. Lord. I didn't even hear you come in."

She forces a smile, but her eyes are all over the place and I can tell she's not going to listen to my response before she even asks the question. "You're home early, so I assume no cavities?"

I ignore the question, and ask one of her instead. "What now?"

I'm sure I don't want to know, but all things considered, I'd rather hear the story from her than the kids at school.

She struggles to meet my eye, twirling her keys with a shaking hand. I see her throat bobbing as she considers what to share, or how to share it. She comes up with six silly words. "His iPad ran out of power."

There is a sardonic edge to her explanation, which I'm not used to. But even she gets frustrated sometimes.

"His iPad ran out of power, right in the middle of reward time, when he'd just reached a new level in his game. He went ballistic." She shakes her head and sighs. "You just never know with the med adjustments if the increases are actually going to help, like they're supposed to, or end up making things *worse*."

I steel myself. "Define ballistic."

"He threw the iPad, and then he eloped."

Eloped.

I've always hated this clinical term, one of the silliest of the bunch, which conjures surprise getaways to Vegas and weddings with Elvis. What it actually means, the way my mom uses it, is that Phillip tried to run away.

"He went out the side of the building, *right* by Route Thirty."

Her eyes look stricken and her throat tightens again as she relays this information. A main route into Philadelphia, Route 30 is a busy two-lane highway with perpetual volume.

"Three staff members took off right after him and got him under control, but you know how fast your brother can run when he's trying to escape."

She covers her eyes with both hands, imagining the worst, the unthinkable. When Phillip's running, Phillip's not paying attention to anything other than getting away. If he'd made it all the way to the road . . .

A moment later she brushes the hair out of her face and raises her chin. She takes a deep breath. Then another. "No sense in thinking about what could have happened, right? He's safe now. That's what's important."

I don't want to think about what could have happened, either. It's awful and I shut it out of my mind as quickly as possible after a quick, silent prayer of thanks for his safety.

"You're going to pick him up?" I ask instead.

She nods. "They felt he was still too agitated to safely ride the bus. This all happened only about twenty minutes ago." She purses her lips and looks at me. "Don't suppose there's any chance you'd want to ride along with me? Keep me company?"

I stare at the floor and shake my head no, shoving aside my

feelings of guilt. Just minutes ago, I'd had the best intentions about going to practice. Now? After my mom's report? No way in hell I'm stepping foot back on campus today.

More gossip. I can count on it.

I close my eyes and say a second silent prayer in thanks that I missed the latest Phillip debacle at Valley Forge High School.

My mom doesn't press the issue. She shifts her purse strap on her shoulder, and wearily steps forward. "Alright. We'll be back soon."

She stops by the door, hand on the knob, calling over her shoulder to me. "I've gotten all of his applications submitted, and put in all the requests to have his records sent. We have two in-take appointments at different schools set up next week, so he won't be in school next Tuesday."

"Do you think one of them will take him?" I ask.

My mom looks back at me, her eyes still haunted. As hard as she's trying not to, I can tell she's picturing the busy road again. "I hope so."

Practice forgotten, I'm into the sour cream and onion Pringles before her wheels have even left the driveway.

I hope the timing of Phillip's elopement left ample opportunity for kids to stand around at their lockers and make "OMG" comments about what they might have witnessed. I hope there was plenty of time in the locker rooms for the football players to re-hash the latest bout of "crazy," and for my teammates to do the same before practice.

The next morning, I'm trying not to worry about Phillip, or

more truthfully, trying not to worry about conversations about Phillip. We have an away game against Lower Merion, and per our usual routine the team is meeting for breakfast at the diner down the road to "fuel up"—Leighton's term—for the day.

It means getting up forty-five minutes earlier than usual, but I typically really like team breakfasts. Erin and I always drive to the diner together, and by the time we leave to head toward school, we're hopped up on team enthusiasm, coffee with lots of sugar and milk, and the lollipops we buy at the counter when we pay our bills. We crank the radio way up as we drive, and I'm always in a great mood by homeroom.

I don't want to think about anyone's stupid comments ruining the tradition.

Erin and I enter the diner as mirror images, both already in uniform, wearing plaid kilts, our matching hoodies, and colored ribbons in our ponytails. It's an added bonus of game day, not having to plan an outfit the night before, knowing we'll be wearing the right thing without even trying.

Leighton has secured the long table in the middle of the main dining room. She is seated at the middle of it, drinking orange juice instead of coffee, with Dana seated to her left. She greets Erin brightly and compliments her new sneakers, but offers me little more than a half smile. I swear she stares at me a second too long as I find a seat down the table.

Instantly, I'm on edge, fearing the worst, that her lukewarm greeting is very purposeful and has something to do with what the guys reported from the playground. I mean, if Jason said anything to Dana, she inevitably reported it back to Leighton.

Then I tell myself to relax. If Leighton heard anything, if

Leighton suspected anything, I'm sure I'd get worse than a weak smile.

I sit down, scoot closer to the table, and order coffee from the waitress. But the playground incident is back in the forefront of my mind, even though I've shoved it out of there countless times already.

I sigh and stare darkly into the oily surface of my coffee when it is set before me. The idea of Alex not loving Leighton doesn't make me feel particularly satisfied. It doesn't mean anything for me, and it doesn't change anything about our situation. Maybe he was just confiding in me as the friend he believes me to be. Maybe he just needed someone trustworthy to unload on.

I draw in a breath as I remember the way he looked at me in the bathroom, and I feel my cheeks flush.

Alex wasn't just unloading. I know it in my gut. I've been ignoring the realization all weekend because I have no idea what to do with it, but I know it all the same.

Through my distracted haze, I order my usual—sesame bagel with cream cheese and a side order of sausage, for protein. Our order arrives within minutes, but I'm still trying to process my feelings about the Alex situation, chewing thoughtfully on my bagel as I stare into space, quiet and checked out.

The chatter around me is loud and vibrant, but even with these factors at play, I hear the words loud and clear through the racket. I don't catch who says them, but I pick up on them right away.

"So I heard the cray-cray kid was at it again yesterday. Does anyone even know his name?"

Before the subject of Phillip is introduced, there are six different conversations taking place. All of a sudden, there is only one topic on the table.

Not that anyone is able to answer the question about Phillip's name, which is sad in and of itself. He doesn't even get a name, just an awful nickname, "the cray-cray kid."

Leighton polishes off her orange juice and slams the glass down on the table. "Yeah, it's getting totally ridiculous," she says. "I'm a senior. I'm sending in my college applications soon. Grades count now. I'm sitting there, trying to finish my calculus test yesterday, look out the window, and see *this* nonsense. Straight out of *One Flew Over the Cuckoo's Nest*, that god-awful old movie we had to watch for psych/soc. People chasing this kid, whoever he is, back and forth across the side green, and he's laughing and grinning like it's some kind of game, before he drops to the floor with his legs in the air, like a bug." She pauses for shock value. "And that was all before he took off his shoes and pants."

My cheeks blaze and I wish I could disappear.

My mom hadn't mentioned the *disrobing*, another stupid clinical term. My instinct told me that Leighton wasn't lying, and that my mother had chosen to spare me some of the gorier details of Phillip's display.

I cringe, picturing his SpongeBob boxers from the laundry basket. What are the chances he wasn't wearing something *totally* mortifying yesterday? What are the chances I can find *any* way to perceive this situation as less than totally mortifying?

"These kids just really don't belong here," Dana speaks up. "I mean, this is supposed to be *the* best school district in the state, right? We're on the cover of *Philadelphia* magazine every year.

But these are the stories that never get talked about. Like how they're allowing the school to be turned into a loony bin."

Leighton nods her head in agreement. "Well, I told my parents about it, for one. And I told Alex to make sure his dad knows exactly what's been happening, too. He's on the school board—he has to be able to do something."

Again, I swear I feel her gaze shift in my direction.

For just one second, I wish I had the balls to look up and meet her head-on.

You don't need to do anything, I want to tell her. *He'll be out of here before you even know. Just let it go.*

There's something else I'd really like to tell her, too.

And Alex will never help you, not the way you want him to.

He's in the process of building a playground for kids with disabilities and she thinks she can rally him to get my brother booted out of school as quickly as possible.

She doesn't know him at all. I remember what he confessed, and just for a second, I allow myself to feel self-satisfied.

But she manages to ruin everything, like always.

As she stands up and pushes in her chair to leave, her shoulders are square and her voice is resolute. "Don't worry about it," she promises Dana. "I'm not going to let this go. I know the parents don't know what's going on, and it's annoying that it's just allowed to happen." She shakes her head. "That'll change."

I am suddenly nauseated. Leighton is determined, and when she is determined, she gets what she wants.

Please let it go, Leighton, I beg silently. *Just please let it go.*

I drag my feet following the crowd to the counter, where we pay our checks one by one. I shake my head when Erin offers me a strawberries-and-cream lollipop and buy a pack of Tums instead.

I'm not in a good mood heading toward homeroom. I have a sick feeling in my stomach that persists all day.

Whispering, by definition, is meant to be both quiet and private. So I suppose there are plenty of people in this world who are able to go about their business, oblivious to when others nearby are whispering to one another.

I'm not one of those people. My whisper radar developed at an early age, right along with my staring monitor. It doesn't matter how low people keep their voices or how they make every attempt at discretion. When people whisper anywhere in my vicinity, I know it.

I'm sitting in the middle of the bus on the way to our game against Lower Merion, with Erin in the seat beside me. Plenty of my teammates are carrying on loud conversations and "Let's Get It Started" is blasting out of a giant boom box right behind us. Neither the chatter nor the pulsing beat can drown out the whispering, though.

I glance over my shoulder toward the seniors in the back of the bus, searching for the source. I see heads bent together, in clusters of twos and threes, hands covering mouths. Every once in a while a head pops up above the seat, meerkat style, before ducking down again. I catch furtive glances and hear giggles that grow too loud before the giggler is promptly shhed.

Yep, I definitely know when someone is being whispered about, and before long, I start to get the sense that that someone is me. I observe without letting on that I'm doing so, and more than once, when I see eyes dart above or around the back seats of the bus, I catch them looking in my direction. My throat turns to sawdust and my stomach turns a somersault.

It's a god-awful feeling, being whispered about.

Before I can think about reaching for the half-eaten pack of Tums in the pouch of my hoodie, I look up to find Leighton hovering above us, holding on to the back of the seat to steady herself on the moving bus.

She smiles sweetly and talks to Erin, but her eyes never leave mine. "Erin, can you switch places with me for a hot minute? I need to talk to Jordyn real quick."

My best friend flies out of the seat without any further consideration of my overall well-being—thank you *so much*, Erin—and Leighton eases down beside me. She is still staring at me, eyes cool and appraising, her mouth a thin, disapproving line.

I've been nervous since the conversation about Phillip this morning, but all of a sudden it occurs to me that Leighton could be here to confront me about something else entirely. Leighton could be here about Alex.

My stomach becomes a U.S. Olympic gymnast competing in a floor routine to take the all-around gold medal.

I take a final look toward the back of the bus, and realize that all attempts at discretion have gone straight out the window. Some girls hang blatantly over seats and the remaining faces peer around the sides of them. Conversations have been abandoned. Everyone is watching, and listening, and it's pretty much my worst nightmare.

Leighton reaches up and adjusts her ponytail, like this is a casual, friendly exchange. "So were you ever going to step up and be honest?"

I am still picturing myself in that Dr. Seuss bathroom, my face only inches from her boyfriend's, and as I fumble for some sort of rational explanation, she catches me off guard with her follow-up.

"Why didn't you speak up this morning?" she demands. "I mean, you could have *said* that I was talking about your brother, for Christ's sake."

My stomach stops in the middle of its tumbling pattern and turns to ice. I feel every last pair of eyes on the back of my head, which feels like it's on fire, in total contrast to the pit of my stomach.

"What do you mean?" I mumble.

Leighton laughs once, a miffed little huff. "What do you *mean*, what do I mean? Again, not trying to be a bitch or anything, but the rest of us have rights, too. I just wanted to find out the kid's name, so I could talk to my parents about the problem. A name's not really a secret, and Mr. Karzanski told me." She pauses and raises her shoulders expectantly. "So? Phillip Michaelson. He's your brother, right? Or at least a cousin or something?"

It's surreal hearing Phillip's full name coming out of Leighton's mouth. Somehow, even in the midst of my worst fears about his presence at my school, I never actually thought I'd be sitting across from her, with his name on her lips.

There's really nothing left to do, nothing left to protect.

So I meet her eyes. "He's my brother."

Her big blue eyes widen, like she was maybe expecting me to refute the information she'd been given. "Seriously? And you didn't speak up when I was going on and on about him this morning? Why wouldn't you say something?" She glances around at all the other girls. "Now I feel like a total idiot."

Like this is about her more than it's about me.

Like she cares, like she regrets how she talked about Phillip.

Even if he weren't my brother, he would be someone's. She hadn't talked about him like a human being, but she sure was putting on a good show now. What a *decent* person Leighton Lyons is.

She crosses her arms on her chest and shakes her head. "I don't get it. I'd never let anyone talk about my family that way."

Leighton has younger twin sisters, Lydia and Lola, who seem just as beautiful and accomplished and perfect as she is. Leighton has no idea.

I refuse to let her shame me and keep my chin up. "It's different," I squeak. I wait until my voice is stronger before speaking again. "It's private."

"With all due respect?" she smirks. "It kinda stopped being private when he started shucking his clothes in full view of my calc class, Jordyn." She shakes her head a final time. "I just wish you'd said something. Like I said, I feel really stupid now, talking about him while his sister was sitting *right there*."

You should feel stupid anyway. It should have felt wrong, the things you were saying, regardless of who was listening.

She stands up before I can respond, before I can actually muster the courage to say the words that are pounding against my temples. She lingers a final moment, staring down at me. "I mean, you're *such* good friends with my boyfriend, right? I don't get why you wouldn't be honest with me."

Leighton gives me a final look before returning to her seat, one that speaks volumes, one that tells me someone has indeed told her about Alex and me at the park. I'm certain she is aware there is plenty I haven't been honest with her about, and she wants me to know that she knows.

I'm suddenly pretty sure that her motive in confronting me on the bus, publicly identifying me as the sister of "the cray-cray kid," has more to do with Alex than it has to do with Phillip.

I'm officially exposed in every sense of the word.

My cheeks on fire with embarrassment, shame, and something akin to fear, I turn to face the seat before me, counting the silent seconds until Leighton has returned to the back of the bus.

It's my worst game of the season. My body is sluggish and clumsy, maybe because my brain is too distracted to effectively coordinate quick and accurate movements. I trip over my feet and allow the ball to be stolen from me. Coach calls for a substitution way before the first half ends, which is something I'm not used to, and I hang my head as I jog off the field.

In contrast to my pitiful performance, Leighton's is stellar. She's on fire on offense, and scores three goals in the same amount of time it takes me to get pulled from the game. Our tense, awkward exchange on the bus seems to have fueled her and depleted me in equal amounts. Which really isn't fair.

I spend the second half of the game sitting the bench and feeling crummy. It's a cold late-fall afternoon, and after working up a sweat when I'm actually *in* the game, my clothes are damp and leave me chilled. I hunch over, trying to warm my hands in the flimsy material of my plaid kilt. I leave them twisted in the material to keep from biting my nails and revealing the frazzled state of my nerves.

I don't even know what to worry about first. I feel my eyes fill, knowing I can't really blame the tears on the sudden wind that is whipping across the open field. I wipe them away before anyone can see because it's not an option to sit here and cry in front of Leighton.

The second half passes, Leighton secures the victory for our squad, and the bulk of the team seems elated as we head back to the bus. I linger near the back of the group and soon realize that one other person seems pretty miserable right along with me. Erin.

Not that she's talking to me, or even looking at me.

When we board the bus, Erin chooses a different seat from the one we shared on the ride here, near the JV players in the front. I'm eager to stay as far away from Leighton as possible, but I suspect something else is motivating Erin's relocation.

She spreads her belongings across the seat—clearly she's not looking for company—but I squeeze myself onto the edge of the seat anyway, my hockey stick bumping my knees every time someone tries to pass us. Erin continues to ignore me, staring gloomily at the back of the vinyl seat in front of us until the engine roars to life and the full bus lumbers forward.

I wait until we are on the highway, and then I turn toward her and put my hand on her forearm. "Erin?"

She twists away and folds her arms over her chest. She still won't look at me. "Is this the real reason why we never hang out at your house? All the other reasons you've said, were they all just lies?"

I inhale a deep breath, thinking before I answer. "Yes and no." I stare down at my lap and start mumbling. "But, yeah, it's really hard to have people over with Phillip there."

The words sound silly coming out, because it's really not difficult to have people around Phillip when he's at home. If he has his headphones on and his gaming system is powered up, he's happy as a clam.

Erin finally looks at me, her eyes hard and appraising. "So *no one* else knew? Not Tanu? Not Alex? How could you honestly keep something like this a secret for so long?"

I ignore her final question, which is much harder to answer. "No one else knew either, Erin."

She tries to give off a careless shrug, but it comes off jerky and agitated. "So I'm no different from anyone else, then. Guess I'm just one more person who didn't know. Guess I shouldn't feel bad then."

"You really shouldn't," I insist. "It wasn't personal. It's about my family, not anybody else."

Erin stares out the window, away from me, but her words still lash like a whip. "Well, I'm sorry, Jordyn, but it feels pretty damn personal. I get why you didn't tell Leighton, or random people. I get why you didn't stand up on the first day of school and broadcast that Phillip was your brother. I know how things work around here, and I don't blame you for that."

She whirls around to face me, and just when I think I can't

possibly feel any worse today, I notice the glassy coat of tears in her eyes. "But this is something you could've told me, something you *should* have told me. You either have no trust in me whatsoever, or else you put absolutely no value in our friendship."

"You don't know how much I just wanted normalcy," I whisper desperately. "You don't know how much I wish we could've hung out at my house, how much I wish it was easier for me to tell someone." I stare sadly at the plaid material of my kilt, and my throat tightens. "I just really didn't want people to see me differently. When I was little—"

"That's stupid." She spits the words out, interrupting me, shaking her head like I'm entirely clueless. "Phillip being your brother wouldn't have made me see you any differently. But I sure see you differently now."

She retrieves her iPod from her pocket and jams pink earbuds into her ears, succinctly ending our conversation.

Chapter Ten

Beep beepbeepbeepbeep! Beep beepbeepbeepbeep!

The next morning, my alarm clock persists in its annoying attempts to rouse me. I roll over, slamming my palm down on the snooze button for the third time.

I roll back onto my side, pull my covers up to my chin, and stare mournfully out the window. I'd fake sick, if it wouldn't just delay the inevitable. The big, convoluted mess of ick would just be waiting for me at school tomorrow.

My mind is twisted with worry and my stomach is in knots because I have too many problems to even begin to separate and prioritize.

My best friend isn't speaking to me. My best friend might even laugh at the term, as she seems to consider our relationship a complete sham now.

The intimidating queen of the senior class called me out on keeping Phillip a secret, and instinct tells me she's aware there is something just below the surface going on between me and her boyfriend.

The knots in my stomach relax, just for a second, to release a wave of sadness.

Her boyfriend. I mean, he's *still* her boyfriend, regardless of what he confessed at the park. I have no idea where he fits in all this, whose side he'll ultimately end up on. Considering the way I fled the scene, what reason does he have to end up on mine?

And I'm officially "Phillip's sister" again. The news is out, and there's no hope of containment. I'm no longer just me. Going forward, at school, I will always be viewed in relation to him and his behavior, and all anyone seems to know about Phillip is sneaker-throwing and stripping. Fabulous.

The sixty-day timeline to find a new placement expires in weeks and my mom sounded optimistic about his acceptance at one or both of the other schools. But what's done is done, and I'm pretty sure I'll always be associated with some element of weirdness now. I don't really see any way to undo that.

At the rate I'm going, I can pretty much count on Phillip having some kind of episode today, just to *really* top things off.

And somehow, I'm supposed to focus on an A.P. History essay test smack-dab in the middle of all this. I didn't get much studying done last night.

I have some pretty shitty luck, I think as I shove my covers back and stomp toward the shower.

I make it to the main lobby at the last possible minute. I stalled as much as I could, taking the time to methodically straighten my hair, even though the day is already damp and rain is forecasted. I took forever getting dressed, finally deciding on a plain black shirt and gray skinny jeans. Best to aim for nondescript, because the last thing I feel like doing today is attracting any more attention. Plus, the colors mirror my mood.

I remember guidance lessons from middle school, when the counselors tried to stress to all of us girls how it was more important to have one *good* friend than a whole lot of fickle friends, and as I walk through the double doors, these words ring very true. If I could at least count on Erin—to sit next to me, to weather the stares at my side—things would seem much easier. More than ever, I regret how I treated our friendship, how I tried to keep it tucked into a separate little compartment of my life and never gave it the room or opportunity to actually blossom and grow.

Erin was right: She always tried to be a good friend to me. Maybe telling her about Phillip wouldn't have changed that. I never gave her the chance, and regardless of how many times she offered to be there for me in the past, today it's too late to ask that of her.

So I walk into the lobby alone. I do my best to keep my chin up and my expression relaxed. I have no idea what people might be saying about me or my family today, but I tell myself that ultimately, the day will pass. Everyone will eventually move on to other things. Who knows where I'll end up, but for now, I just have to get through the day.

I walk down the steps, heading toward the group of junior girls. No one even glances up. Everyone is huddled in small groups, heads together, whispering. My automatic assumption is that the whispering is about me again, but as the bell rings and the wave of students moves toward homeroom, the fragmented comments I pick up on don't seem to fit.

"Last night . . . over the phone . . ."

"Not really . . . I heard she doesn't want to talk about it . . ."

"No . . . pretty sure . . . said he already changed his Facebook status . . ."

What on earth are they talking about? What news has trumped the revealing of Phillip's family ties?

I don't get any answers during the morning. Then I head to history class and have other things to worry about, namely, the test I'm unprepared for and the uncertainty of how Alex will treat me.

But he doesn't really treat me any way at all. He rushes in as the bell sounds and won't make eye contact. His eyes are dark and stormy, and his mouth is set in a scowl. An awful feeling enters my stomach as he slams his book bag onto the desk and collapses into the seat behind me without even saying hello.

Then our test packets are handed out and the room is silent for the remainder of the period. I don't have any further opportunity to investigate his mood.

My concentration is shot.

His behavior answers my question about whose side he's ended up on.

I attempt to focus, wishing I could talk to him, but I never get the chance. I have to stay ten minutes into the lunch period to finish my test, and he's out the door the moment the bell rings.

I really don't feel like walking into the cafeteria, certainly not this late, after everyone else is already there. But internally repeating my mantra about only delaying the inevitable by avoiding it, I tighten my grip on my paper-bag lunch, and stride purposefully toward our table. Erin is noticeably absent, but my seat beside Tanu is still open.

I feel a smidgen of relief as I sit down and she offers me a quick smile. She seems rather oblivious, which is strange. Again I find myself wondering if the news about Phillip being my brother has truly been overshadowed by something bigger.

I unwrap my sandwich. "Where's Erin?" I ask cautiously.

"She's doing a test review with some people from her French class. I dunno. Weird."

Tanu is distracted and I can tell she's leaning to her right, keeping one ear toward the middle of the table. The girls from my grade are still whispering together instead of having a normal lunchtime conversation. They have their backs turned to the guys, who are carrying on as normal. With the exception of Alex, that is, who glowers down at his meatball sandwich instead of eating it. Sometimes he turns his angry stare toward the gaggle of whispering girls, shaking his head before dropping his gaze again.

That's it. I have to ask the question out loud.

"What the heck is going on around here today?"

Tanu finally gives me her full attention, and her eyes widen in surprise. They hold a trace of excitement, because Tanu loves sharing gossip. "Oh my God, I assumed he told you. That you would know, of all people."

"Know what?"

She glances toward the end of the table, then twists around

in her seat to whisper into my ear. "So people are saying that Alex broke up with Leighton."

It's just about the last thing I expect to hear and I'm too surprised to react, to feel much of anything about this news. It all comes together—the murmurings about changes in Facebook status . . . Alex's mood in class . . . maybe that wasn't about me, after all.

Tanu awaits a reaction.

"Seriously?"

She nods, adamant. "Yeah. No one's really confirmed it, because I don't think Leighton's talking about it, but you know, stuff gets out. I think they had some big fight last night."

"About what?"

Tanu shrugs, and digs her fork back into her Rubbermaid container. "Don't know. Trying to find out." She returns to leaning toward the middle of the table, only pretending to eat her lunch as she tries to get the rest of the story.

I struggle to eat, too. Between my late arrival and the unexpected news, I barely manage to choke a couple of bites down. I can't really wrap my head around it. Alex and Leighton being together caught me totally off guard, but the sudden demise of their relationship is even more startling.

But as the junior class exits the cafeteria and the senior class filters in, there is a very noticeable distance between Alex and Leighton. They make no attempt to close it, and they definitely don't look at each other. Leighton laughs loudly with her friends, without a care in the world, and Alex just stares stoically ahead as he marches forward with his teammates.

The rumors are clarified, once and for all, in the locker room before practice.

Leighton climbs atop one of the low benches, clad only in her cobalt sports bra and mesh shorts. She claps twice and then stands there, hands on her hips, staring down in challenge at the group. Her eyes are narrowed into slits, and her mouth is a flat line. She doesn't bother with preliminaries.

"I best not hear anyone talking behind my back. I don't get down with that, okay? You want to know what happened, fine." She lifts and lowers her shoulders once—she is thin enough that I can make out her ribs with this slight movement. "Alex and I broke up. Big whoop. People break up every day around here. Now, moving on."

She hops off the bench and finishes dressing. Within moments, she is talking a mile a minute with Dana and Jamie.

I observe her out of the corner of my eye. Something is off. The thing that I always ruefully admired about Leighton was the authenticity of her confidence, which came off as more than bravado. What I see now is not confidence. It's a show. I sense that Leighton is hurting, and it's no fun watching someone hurting, even if she's not the nicest person in the world.

Since the start of the school year, I've been forced to think about how much it would suck to lose Alex from my life, and it seems she's experiencing that loss now. Maybe she did really care about him, even if she had a different way of showing it. It's hard not to sympathize, just a little bit.

Then practice starts.

Midway through a drill, Jamie's stick somehow gets caught under my feet, and I end up sprawled out on the ground, the wind knocked out of me.

When transitioning to the next activity, Leighton calls me out, loudly, for not hustling, even though I'm right in the middle of the pack.

Then I'm replaced in the starting lineup for the scrimmage. Given that it's two days before a game, I have a feeling I'm losing my starting position for the remainder of the season.

I know my performance in our last game was atrocious, but Leighton's decision to "switch things up" has a personal edge, there's no doubt about it.

Things go from bad to worse when I emerge from a bathroom stall after getting changed and find Leighton and Dana waiting for me. "Come into the lobby with us for a minute?" Leighton asks, even though it's not really a question.

I swallow hard and follow them, ending up in the dimly lit lobby with my back against a wall. They stand in front of me, arms linked casually, like this is going to be a friendly exchange. Somehow I doubt that.

"Like I said earlier," Leighton starts, "I don't like stuff going on behind my back. So . . . I just want you to know I know."

She slides her arm from Dana's—who, for the record, seems to have no purpose there whatsoever other than making sure the odds aren't even—and reaches up to tighten her ponytail. "I don't even know *what* I know, but for the record, I *do* know. Nobody makes me look stupid, okay? And that's what you two are doing." Her eyes harden, and I know that she will never be nice to me again. Not for show. Not at all.

It's a terrifying feeling, having *that* girl at school turn on you so obviously, like being thrown to the wolves. I feel like I'd do anything not to have their teeth at my back.

"I don't get it," she says, "but I say *one* little thing to Alex about the situation with your brother here at school, and suddenly I'm the bad guy. Suddenly, he's breaking up with me." She shakes her head and huffs. "I have to believe it's about more than that, more than him having such a strong reaction to this idea of me 'picking on people who don't deserve it.' I know what a fucking Good Samaritan he is and everything, but there's no way he got that fired up about my suggestion we actually do something about these kids being in our school. No *way*. There has to be more going on here."

I have to speak up, because she's wrong. She's just *wrong*. I've never come close to crossing any lines with Alex. The truth is, I've barely had the nerve to even think about it.

"There's not. I don't . . . I didn't even talk to Alex today, so I have no idea, but, Leighton, I swear to you . . . it's not like—"

"I'm not going to let people make me look stupid, Jordyn," she cuts me off bluntly. "Like I said, I don't know what it's about, but I'm not an idiot. And the more times you stand in front of me and *lie to my face* and act like you have no idea what I'm talking about, the worse you're making it for yourself when I eventually get proof that I'm right. It's pretty stupid on your part. Just thought that should be known." She gives me a final stare, and then tugs on Dana's arm, leading her back toward the locker room. "Have fun with my boyfriend," she calls over her shoulder. "Hope he's worth it."

It sounds like a threat. I'm pretty sure it is.

I stay in the dark, pressed against that wall for a long time, shaky and upset. When I finally manage to move, my legs feel like Jell-O and my hands are trembling at my sides.

This is way worse than people knowing I'm Phillip's sister. The last thing I want is to spend the remainder of the school year with the girls from the senior class turned against me because of the misconception that I was involved in Leighton and Alex's breakup. I hadn't even heard about it, for crying out loud!

I retrieve my belongings from the empty locker room and slam my locker shut. The Phillip situation and the Alex-Leighton situation are, on one hand, unrelated. On the other hand . . . they're not. Phillip coming to my school started the whole chain of events. If Phillip had never come here, Leighton never would have been bothered by his presence. She never would have said anything to Alex, and he never would have broken up with her.

And I never would have fallen victim to a set of circumstances that were beyond my control in the first damn place. I'd still be flying under the radar. As it stands now, I feel like I have a huge bull's-eye on my back.

It's not fair.

I exit the locker room through the parking-lot door. It's dark outside and the sky is spitting; I huddle inside my unsubstantial windbreaker against the wet chill. As I hurry toward my car, I make out another lingerer in the lot: Alex, tossing his equipment into the backseat of his car, which is parked in the row behind mine. As I get closer, I see his expression still looks sour. He's sort of scary looking in general, like a boxer, in baggy sweatpants and a sweatshirt with the hood up.

But he looks up and turns to me as I approach, and I detect

the tiniest of smiles in the shadows of his hoodie. "Hey, M.J.," he greets me tiredly.

It's encouraging and I exhale a huge sigh of relief. Maybe his mood in history class didn't have anything to do with me after all.

"How are you doing?"

He averts his eyes before answering me. "Pretty crappy day." He taps his fist against the driver's-side window, shakes his head, and laughs once, mirthlessly. "Being talked about all damn day . . . it's a lot of fun."

"I'm sorry about that," I respond, fiddling nervously with the frayed strap of my book bag. I didn't expect the topic of his very recent breakup to be out in the open like this.

He turns toward me, leaning against the side of his car, squinting into the light rain. "Well, shit happens. Hopefully people will lose interest soon."

I'm worried that's not going to be the case, at least not as far as Leighton letting me off the hook.

I clear my throat, hemming and hawing a bit before I'm able to spit out anything resembling a coherent sentence. "Alex . . . look, umm . . . Leighton, she told me part of the reason you . . . you know . . . was because she brought something up about Phillip." I shake my head frantically and my words tumble out faster. "I appreciate you being nice about the whole thing and maybe trying to look out for me and my family in some way, but you didn't . . . you don't have to do that."

He stares back at me, expression unreadable, and I babble on, uncertain of the territory I'm stumbling into.

But I continue anyway, thinking about how I just lost my position on the team in a flash, thinking about all the ways she can turn my social life hellish. I can't do third grade all over again. By high school, girls have developed tactics way nastier than forming clubs against one another. Next to Leighton, Caroline's antics seem like child's play.

"Please don't break up with her because of me . . . because of Phillip. She's blaming *me*, Alex, and I . . . I just really don't want that."

Alex's eyes don't stay expressionless for long. They widen in surprise and then I see the surprise morph into a low, seething anger that's unfamiliar and unexpected. His hands ball into fists at his sides and his upper body stiffens. "Are you joking?"

I feel heat work its way into my chilled cheeks. Maybe I'm off base here. Maybe Leighton set me up to look like an idiot in front of him, and maybe their breakup had nothing to do with me whatsoever. I might be reading this all wrong.

I backpedal frantically. "Oh . . . oh . . . I'm an idiot." My palm goes to my forehead and I wince in embarrassment. "I don't mean to pry into your business. She said . . . and I thought . . . but if it had nothing to do with your conversation, or me, I'll butt the hell out."

I offer half a smile, but Alex's eyes only darken further, and the muscle in his jaw twitches with irritation.

"Jesus Christ, Jordyn, can we please have an honest conversation for once?" he explodes. "My God, don't act like you don't know. I wasn't *alone* at the playground." When I just stand there, silent, he throws his hands up and pushes his hood back. "Of course it has to do with you. It *is* about you in a way you seem to be completely freakin' clueless about!"

I am frozen, shell-shocked, as his loud voice reverberates in the empty lot.

Alex takes a step toward me and I can feel the angry energy pulsing around his body. "I told you I wasn't in love with her." His eyes pierce mine. "And I'm pretty sure you know the other side to that story, even if we never talk about it. You know there's no way I could ever sit there and let her try to get at you or your family. But *come on*, Jordyn." He pauses and takes a deep breath. "Don't act like you don't know that this breakup had a lot less to do with the type of person she is than the type of person I think *you* are."

I panic as he wrenches the lid off Pandora's box. "Alex, don't—"

But he's on a tear and I don't think he even hears me. He kind of looks like he wants to throttle me, actually.

"You didn't give me a chance to finish the other day. You took off like you always do." He shakes his head. "Sometimes I really don't get you, you know that? Most people try to make themselves look better on the outside than they really are on the inside. People like Leighton. Then there's you. It's like it's the other way around, like you don't want people to notice what's special about you. You pull away every time they try to." Some of the anger dissipates in his expression and I think I can see a trace of the Alex I know . . . and love . . . again.

"Why doesn't anyone know the girl who chose to work at Camp Hope last summer? Why doesn't anyone know how you went out of your way to make the bathroom at the playground special? It's like you hide that person away and it's *sad*, Jordyn."

My chest constricts and my throat tightens, but if Alex notices, he still doesn't let up on me.

"So I just want to be honest for a minute," he finishes quietly. "You were special." His eyes meet mine and they look pained. "You *are* special. But for whatever reason, you don't want me to acknowledge that. You won't let me close enough to. Why?"

A lump rises in my throat and I feel sudden tears against my lower lashes. My voice is a hoarse whisper, because if I try to out-and-out speak, the tears will surely garble my words. "You remember getting noticed in the wrong way more than you remember getting noticed in the right way, you start just wanting to blend in. You start not wanting to be noticed at all."

The emotions of the week—the embarrassment, the shame, the fear—consume me and the tears crest and break over my cheeks.

Alex reaches up, brushing a tear away with the pad of his thumb. His voice is low and soft. "Yeah, well, too bad I've always noticed you. From day one. I noticed the way the sun changes the color of your eyes." He smiles, remembering. "I noticed the way your skin smells like cinnamon and sugar on warm afternoons. I noticed the way your voice sounded when you talked to your campers, how patient it was, how it calmed them."

His throat tightens and the pain in his eyes is familiar. It's the same pain I've seen reflected in the mirror every time I've allowed myself to think of how I've missed him.

"I noticed how easily our hands fit together the one time you let me touch you. I noticed that you seemed lonely, really, really lonely, even though I didn't know why." His eyelashes flutter as his eyes meet mine. "Which is the most ridiculous thing in the world, considering how badly someone wants to spend time with you. Every single day."

I close my eyes against the crippling onslaught of emotion and feel new tears spill down my face.

"I guess I understand why you walked away last year." Alex shakes his head. "But there's nothing to hide anymore and there's no reason to. If you had a chance to do things differently . . . look me in the eye and tell me you wouldn't take it."

When I don't answer right away, he grasps both my biceps, bringing me even closer, and my eyes fly open. His voice becomes insistent. "Be honest. I know you told me you didn't want that choice, last summer in the closet." His lips press together in frustration and his eyes are demanding. "Look me in the eye and tell me, right now, that you wouldn't choose differently."

I think of how many times my heart has nearly split in half with aching and regret. I consider the power of my memories of last summer, how they badger me, and still hurt over a year later. I feel the energy it takes, every day, to push the feelings away, to keep the words locked behind my lips, to fight the magnetic draw I have toward this boy.

I want to hold his hand. I want to touch his face. I want to memorize his expression when he's sleeping, all over again. I want to feel the pressure of his lips against mine.

I just want him.

But I didn't have the option of choosing differently then. He's asking me to make that choice *now*. Now, I can't shake the more recent memory of the nasty expression on Leighton's face in the silent lobby and her very thinly veiled threat. And I'm terrified of her.

I'm terrified of being treated like a leper again.

I'm terrified of gaining attention not only as "Phillip's sister," but as the girl who stole Leighton's boyfriend. I'm scared of the cruelty that will ensue, because I know how cruel people can be.

Being with Alex would kill all the good between us. Other people's gossip would tarnish all those things that are special about me and Alex.

Why does loving someone always have to hurt?

The risk just seems bigger than the reward.

I push my hair off my forehead and look up at him. "You can't ask me now, Alex. It really doesn't matter what I want. It doesn't matter what the truth is. It would look so bad." My voice drops off. "She'd make my life miserable."

"You care more about what everyone else thinks about you than what I think about you." His response comes out like pieces of ice being chipped off a block. "You care more about that than you care about me." He grimaces and shakes his head. "When someone's presence in your life is difficult, you just pretend them away, don't you? Me . . . your brother . . . it's freakin' sad."

I hang my head and a few final tears make their way toward the pavement. "I know," I admit.

"You know, Leighton, she's far from perfect, but at least she has the backbone to go after what she wants. Nothing scares her." Alex waits until I look up before hammering away at his point. "At least she's honest.

"So maybe it didn't work out, and it turns out the way she

acts doesn't make her a good person, or at least the right person, for me." He looks at me, truly lost. "But if you *are* a good person and have nothing but excuse after excuse to give me . . . then I guess maybe you're not the right person for me, either."

Alex shakes his head and pulls his keys from his pocket. His voice is gentle at first. "You know how I felt about you. You know how I *feel* about you." Then he looks up and his expression and his tone harden all over again. "It's a damn shame you're gonna let all that go to waste just because it's not entirely easy. It's a shame . . . for both our sakes."

He shrugs dismissively and opens his door to climb inside. "Later."

And then he's gone.

Chapter Eleven

Alex is done with me.

He's made his point and spoken his mind. For the rest of the week, he doesn't seem to be changing it, either. He doesn't talk to me and goes out of his way to avoid me, or at least that's how it seems. He's super busy, anyway—the playground opens on Saturday—and he's got plenty to occupy his mind besides me and my utter stupidity. Then he's absent on Friday, making last-minute preparations at the playground.

When I see Leighton at practice, I consider the irony. Despite the vast differences between us, we both ended up in the same boat—without Alex.

But I had a choice. He gave me one. If she hadn't just threatened me . . . if I'd been prepared to hear him say the words out loud . . . if I could have, just for once, been brave. . . .

Not that it matters now. Alex is done with me. My paralysis cost me everything.

Between the Phillip elopement incident on Monday, my fight

with Erin on Tuesday, my numerous confrontations with Leighton, and the parking lot blowup with Alex, I am completely worn out by Thursday. I finish out the week in a fog, limping across the finish line to Friday. I only half concentrate in class and barely talk.

At least Erin is speaking to me again, but just barely. Her eyes remain cold, our exchanges are formal, and I still don't know what will come of our friendship.

I pass on Tanu's invitation to ride along with her and Erin to the away football game. A car ride with Erin doesn't sound like a whole lot of fun. And I don't even want to think about how it would feel to sit in the stands and watch Alex on the field.

It would hurt to look at him. It hurts to even think about him right now.

Everything Alex said was true. Even more than it hurts to think about Alex, it hurts to think about myself—what I've let slip away because I'm too weak, too scared. Because I don't want to hurt any more than I have to.

As I drive home on Friday, something startling occurs to me. Nobody has made a big deal about Phillip being my brother. Maybe Leighton didn't spread the news too far, either because Alex chastised her about it or because the breakup stole her attention.

But it's obvious some people know, and that word is slowly getting around school, because a few of my classmates have approached me about it. Their joint reaction is largely underwhelming. Mostly they just ask me some basic questions and then change the subject. A few even express compassion—"That must be really hard." No one is treating me any different, though. It doesn't feel like elementary school all over again. Maybe that's because it isn't.

I'm starting to feel stupid.

Really stupid.

I'm not sure why things are so much different now than they were when Phillip and I were younger. Maybe the autism awareness movement, all those ribbons with the colorful puzzle pieces, has been more effective in promoting understanding than I give it credit for. Perhaps everyone's a little more mature, or the kids at my new school are different from the kids at my old school. Perhaps everyone is just too busy with their own lives to be all that concerned with mine. Maybe I'm the only one with the hyperfocus on Phillip.

Maybe not all of us are stuck back in third grade.

But I never considered that it could be like this, that the only person who'd make such a big deal about Phillip being my brother would be . . . *me*.

This realization nags at me, leaving me more exhausted than ever. I'm having trouble looking at myself in the mirror.

So when my mom mentions that her college roommate and husband are staying in downtown Philly for business, I do something nice instead. I offer to stay home with Phillip so my parents can enjoy a meal out and catch up with old friends.

My mom brushes off her evident surprise, which quickly turns into elation. She seems reinvigorated as she dashes out the door thirty minutes later, wearing makeup *and* perfume, her hair down. I remember how my mom's week started out with a phone call that her youngest child had nearly run into traffic. She's much happier now and full of optimism about a new school placement that sounds like it's going to come through.

It cheers me up to see her happy and I smile at the knowledge that my actions can make *someone* happy these days. Otherwise . . . all around . . . I seem to be failing at that.

Phillip's easy to babysit. I can whip up Annie's rice pasta and cheese with one hand tied behind my back, since it's one of the only things he ever eats. I order a pizza for myself, and we eat side by side on the couch.

I tug on the wire of his gaming system. "Turn off Nintendo, Phillip. Pick a movie?" I encourage him.

He scans the shelves. "*Scoundrels.*"

He's referring to *Dirty Rotten Scoundrels.* We've watched it a hundred times. "*Three Amigos*?" I suggest.

Phillip has this weird affinity for Steve Martin, whose antics he seems to find absolutely hilarious.

"*Scoundrels!*"

I'm not going to win this one, so I stand up and retrieve the disc. "Okay, Phillip. You win. *Scoundrels* it is."

"I've got culture coming out of my ass." He recites from the film, his inflection spot-on.

I bend over to insert the DVD, hiding my face so he doesn't see I'm laughing. I'm supposed to discourage his cursing, but sometimes it's pretty damn funny.

I sit back down beside him, paper plate on my lap, and listen to the familiar musical opening of the movie. At one point about an hour later, when Steve Martin's character's wheelchair rolls into a pool, Phillip looks over at me while laughing. He keeps eye contact for nearly fifteen seconds and it's possible to believe we're actually laughing together rather than just in the same space.

Phillip shuts off the movie at eight thirty, right in the middle of a scene. "Good night. Sleep tight. Don't let the bedbugs bite." Our mom used to say it every night when we were little, and Phillip's held on to the rhyme. He heads upstairs without looking at me again or waiting for a response. He always goes to bed early, a combined result of his medication regimen and just how tiring it is being Phillip.

Then it's really quiet in our house and I riffle through our DVD collection, looking for something that might interest me. Most of our collection's devoted to Phillip—way too many Steve Martin comedies, SpongeBob collections, and his expansive collection of cartoons and video games. After the week I've had, I don't want anything romantic *or* sad either.

As I flip through the discs, a case falls off the shelf. It's thinner than the rest, homemade. I turn it over to read the label.

Five excited words leap off the case, written in black Sharpie, all caps.

HE SPEAKS—PHILLIP, AGE FOUR!!!!!

There is something momentous captured in the title, in the surplus of exclamation points, and I slide the disc into the player and wait for it to load.

A moment later, a grainy shot of our old dining room comes into view, making me instantly nostalgic as I take in the scratched wooden table and the autumn table runner adorned with turkeys and pumpkins, which didn't make the move to our new house.

There is Phillip, scrawny as ever, seated atop both a pillow and a prickly plastic therapy cushion to help sustain his focus and help him reach the table. My mom is seated to his left, looking much younger than she does now, yet older at the same time, thanks to the outdated hairstyle captured on film.

There is a pained look on her face, because as the video opens, Phillip has both hands over his ears, his eyes are clenched shut, and he is screaming. It is high-pitched and repetitive, like a siren. Yet my mom's lips remain pinched in determination between quiet prompts to my brother.

The scene brings back memories of Phillip's early intervention services, how he was forced to endure speech therapy four times a week. The therapist would come to our house and I was bribed with cheddar popcorn and extra time in front of the Disney Channel to stay out of the way so that my mom was free to observe the therapist's techniques and any progress Phillip might demonstrate. Typically, there wasn't any.

Sometimes I watched my mom as she watched like a hawk, taking copious notes so that she was later able to replicate the therapy sessions and the demands included within. After the therapist left, and after we ate dinner, she would pick up where they left off, working tirelessly, even as Phillip fought her every step of the way.

Phillip had never wanted to talk to any of us. It took us over three years to realize he was even capable of producing speech, when he finally started screaming the word "no!" about anything and everything, hands locked firmly over his ears.

Somehow his single-word protest translated into some sort

of victory for my mother, and the language interventions became more intensive.

The twenty-minute video is painful to watch, because for every step forward, it's two steps back.

My mother gently taps the laminated picture symbol on the table before them. It bears an image of Polly-O string cheese, Phillip's dietary staple at the time. "Phillip wants . . . ," she prompts.

"Nooooooooooooo!" he screams, then begins shrieking again and slides off his seat like a limp noodle.

My mom appears unfazed. "First chair, then cheese," she says, once, twice, three times, always calm, until Phillip manages to collect himself and returns to the table. He is rewarded with a tiny piece of cheese, but the real prize, the whole stick, remains beside my mother.

She holds it up and taps the picture again. "Phillip wants . . ."

He doesn't scream this time but begins pounding his temples with his fists. He hits himself hard, likely producing red marks, but if my mom is upset, she doesn't let it show. She slowly pries his fingers open and spreads them on the table. "Soft hands," she says calmly, "then cheese."

When Phillip keeps his hands away from his head, he is given another small piece of cheese.

This goes on for another fifteen minutes as Phillip tries to escape the demand of saying a single word with every trick in his arsenal. My mom never gives up, shaping every small, acceptable behavior along the way—soft hands, bottom in seat, eyes on me.

Finally, she gives the prompt one more time and taps the picture. "Phillip wants . . ."

"Cheese."

The word comes out clearly and easily. As a frustrated observer eleven years later, someone who knows my brother very well, I still can't help wondering why he didn't save everyone the trouble and just say the damn word in the first place, if he knew how.

In the video, my mother is visibly stunned. She looks toward my father, behind the camera, in surprise. Her face breaks into a wide smile as she asks him, "Did you get it? Please *God*, tell me you're still filming."

Obviously, there were many takes when Phillip had *not* produced the word "cheese."

"I got it." I hear my dad's voice. "Now give him his cheese!"

"Oh, right!" My mom laughs, still giddy, and hands Phillip the entire stick of cheese.

"Cheese," he says happily, removing the plastic and licking the stick up and down. "Cheese. Cheese."

I shake my head as the camera is turned off and the screen turns to static.

There's only one video, but there could have been thousands like it. Every single word, skill, and milestone was earned upon a battlefield. My mom and dad fought for every *single* skill Phillip mastered. The battles took years, and the victories were conceded eons after they should have been.

As I put the DVD in the case and slide it carefully back onto the shelf, I think about where I fit in the context of these battles. I was left alone, a lot, in the application of their concept of fairness. There's no denying this—I just saw the proof of it on the screen—and somewhere deep down, I can still detect the roots of resentment.

On the other hand, I'm well aware of another video that exists, and it's probably stored upstairs in my big box of accomplishments. In it, I'm almost a year younger than Phillip was in the video I just suffered through. I'm a precocious three-year-old, dressed in a satiny teal-blue skirt with purple mermaid fins, belting out "Part of Your World" from *The Little Mermaid*. I sing it a capella, word for word, never missing a beat. I sing it with ease.

Someone had cared enough to videotape it. Someone had been watching, likely applauding, likely assuring me that, yes, one day I'd end up playing Ariel on Broadway. Phillip had just received his diagnosis around that time, but someone still made time for Disney princess dress-up and videotaped my performance.

Being left alone for thirty minutes at a time isn't the exact same thing as being neglected. The scales may have never been tipped in my favor, but I guess they weren't perpetually out of balance, either.

The next morning, apprehensive but resolved, I dress slowly. I'm not sure my presence will be welcomed at the playground opening, but I still want to be there. I want to see Alex's hard work recognized and I want to be one more person there to acknowledge his efforts. I'll stay in the background.

I stare out the back window—the sunlight is faint and a few colorful leaves are already on the ground. I button my fitted plaid boyfriend shirt, hoping the sun makes a more noticeable appearance at the playground site.

A squirrel catches my attention as he prances gracefully along the top bar of our old playground set. I stare at the swings. The paint is patchy, and the whole thing is rusted and rickety, but we've never gotten rid of it. It still gets use, although I haven't been on it in at least six years. Phillip, however, at age fifteen, still loves to swing. You can find him out there, regardless of season, regardless of temperature. It soothes him, swinging, the consistent back and forth he can always count on.

A thought pops into my head, and I go find my mom, who is drinking coffee in the kitchen. "So I'm going to the opening for Alex's playground project," I tell her as I pull on my North Face fleece. "And . . . I was thinking maybe Phillip would like to come with me."

The mug in her hand freezes midway to her mouth. "Really?"

"Yeah. Why not?"

I can see her mind churning away, wondering at what point during the week an alien invaded her daughter's body, rendering her a more giving, supportive family member.

Ultimately, she shakes her head and drains her coffee. "I don't know, honey. I don't want him to give you any problems."

"He won't give me any problems. There's an awesome swing set there and it's brand-new. We won't stay long, he'll swing, and then we'll come home. I *have* driven Phillip places before," I remind her.

Not a lot, because I never really want to . . . but I've done it. She rises from her stool. "Maybe if I come along, too . . ."

I put my hand up to stop her. "I can handle it. It's only ten minutes away. If there's any real problem, I'll call you."

I turn my back on her before she can protest further and walk into the living room, where I find Phillip on the couch, giggling while watching the Cartoon Network.

"Hi, Phillip," I interrupt, voice not too loud, not too quiet. "Would Phillip like to swing?" I make sure to keep my language simple. "Try new swings?"

He looks up and stares at me for a minute, eyes distant and pensive. "Would you trust a shifty-eyed moose?" he asks seriously.

I have no idea what he's referencing or where he heard the question, but I tell him, no, I would not, and he stands up. I take this as a yes, and hand him his favorite red sweatshirt to put on over his T-shirt.

Before we head to the car, I make sure I have the tote containing his Bose headphones, his Nintendo 3DS, and several snack bags of gluten-free pretzel sticks. He occupies himself with his game on the ride, but when we pull into the lot and he glimpses the impressive spread of the playground before him, he abandons it at once. He doesn't even reach for his headphones as he opens the car door. He is out like a flash and makes a beeline for the colorful set of swings to the left of the playground.

There are a ton of kids already on the equipment, and I follow Phillip as he joins the fray. He selects a swing on the end and is airborne within seconds. I stand back and watch, unconcerned. There are kids of all ages and disabilities—some even older than Phillip who look like they should've outgrown playgrounds but appear among the most excited—and he does not stand out in this crowd. If he yells, if he flails, if he swings for two hours without pause, the kids and families around him will remain unfazed.

There seems to be a general understanding among the children and teens in the group—you've got your issues and I've got mine. Your issues aren't a big deal to me.

It's a nice feeling, one I'm very grateful Alex helped cultivate. Regret squeezes my heart in its strong, inescapable grasp.

I keep my eyes on my brother, willing the sad feelings away. He is happy here, and this makes me smile. I realize there's not always an inverse relationship between his happiness and mine. I just wish that Phillip's playground expanded beyond this space. I wish the scope of his happiness was broader, that it came easier.

At eleven o'clock, Phillip is still content, which I'm thankful for, so I can attend the small ceremony taking place on the colorful wooden bridge between the two big sections of the jungle gym. The mayor gives a speech, thanking all the participants who helped bring the playground to life. Prominent fund-raisers and representatives from the charity organizations that contributed are front and center, but so is Alex. He is given special recognition and is the only person on the bridge who draws a standing ovation from the crowd. His mom rings a cowbell from her wheelchair, which is positioned right at the base of the bridge.

Alex's cheeks are pink and he smiles humbly toward the ground, but I can detect the pride in his expression. Everything else about him looks exhausted, from the slump of his shoulders to the unfamiliar shadows under his eyes, and it's obvious how stressful his past few days have been, separate from the stress I added to them.

I long to hug him in a way I haven't even allowed myself to think about in over a year, an outdated yearning from those sticky summer afternoons sitting beside him on the picnic table at the club. I wish I could gather him in my arms and let his tired forehead rest on my shoulder. I would whisper in his ear exactly how proud of him I am.

The desire is all-consuming and crippling. Alex opened the door to my feelings that I'd closed, and this time I can't seem to shut it again. I shove my hands into my pockets and stare uselessly into space.

Someone jostles my arm, pulling me from my sad daydream.

I turn and I'm surprised to find Erin at my side, red hair glistening against the collar of her bright green peacoat.

"Hey," I greet her tentatively. "I didn't know you were coming out this morning."

Our communication is definitely hurting these days.

She smiles in Alex's direction. "Oh, I wanted to come out and give him some support. I felt bad I couldn't help on the workday."

"That's really nice of you."

As I look around at the crowd, I realize not too many kids from school are here. Some people from our classes and some other members of the football team, yes. But mostly, now that the playground is up and running, it's families and kids. People were willing to pitch in and help when Alex asked for it, but it doesn't seem like it crossed too many people's minds to show up today.

But Erin is thoughtful enough to come, which makes me feel worse than ever.

We both end up staring at the ground, silent.

"I'm really sorry, Erin," I spit out breathlessly. "I just want you to know that. I have a lot of regrets right now. Some people aren't going to let me do anything about them, but maybe some people will." I glance at her from the corner of my eye, hopeful.

She takes a minute to respond, and I follow her gaze. She is watching a mother help her daughter clean up. Even though the girl must be about our age, she has spilled bright red juice down the front of her shirt and sports a juice mustache above her lip. The girl is dressed like a much younger child, and her pigtails are pinned up with colorful hair ties. She shrieks loudly and jumps up and down while her mom tries to clean her.

"It can be kind of embarrassing at times," I whisper. "It can get in the way. But it never took away from me *wanting* to be your friend."

Erin inhales sharply, still watching the interaction between the girl and her mother. Erin, who is forever picking apart her own image, who never seems satiated when it comes to the approval of others. "I get it," she answers. She twists to look at me. "I was hurt, but this wasn't about me. I knew that; it just sucks being lied to. In whatever sense of the word."

"I'm sorry," I repeat.

"Like I said, I get it, and if you want to . . ." A real smile finally appears, one I haven't seen from her in a while. ". . . then, hell yeah, of course I still want to be your friend."

Relieved, I smile in response, and I reach for her hand to give it a quick squeeze. "Cool. Thanks."

I glance toward the swings, suddenly remembering that I haven't checked in on Phillip in a few minutes. He still looks happy as a clam and I take a deep breath. "You know . . . my brother's actually here today. If you want to meet him."

My heart hammers, conditioned with fear, but I manage to propose the introduction.

She nods and follows me toward the swings. "What should I say to him?"

"Just say 'hi.' He'll probably say 'hi' back. He's calmer when he swings." I grin. "Then be prepared, he might ask you if you'd trust a shifty-eyed moose."

Erin shrugs mildly. "Of course; who wouldn't?"

I crack up and, feeling impulsive, offer an invite. I haven't cleared it with my parents, but I know they won't mind. They'll be surprised as heck, but they won't mind. "You want to come over later? Hang out?"

Her eyes light up, and again I feel bad about how easy it would have been to set our friendship on a different path. "Yeah. Absolutely!"

We stand on the edge of the swing area. I know better than to actually interrupt Phillip's swinging, so I call to him from the ground. "Phillip, this is my friend Erin. Say hi, Phillip."

He whizzes by us, pumping his legs. "Hi, Phillip."

Erin smiles. "It's good to meet you, Phillip."

He passes us again on his way back toward the sky. "Hi, Phillip."

I turn to her and shrug. "That might be the best we're gonna get."

"That's okay, you tried. He tried." Then her gaze drifts over my shoulder and she nudges me with her elbow. "I think your buddy wants to talk to you anyway."

I turn and look, and the hammering in my heart escalates to a whole new level.

Alex. He's dressed in a drab olive-green Boy Scout button-down with an American flag patch on the chest and his troop number on the left sleeve, jeans, work boots, and a navy down vest. He is staring at me, but he's too far away for me to read anything in his eyes. His expression is flat. If it's an invitation, it's not a very warm one.

Then I look back at Erin, realizing that her expression is sort of knowing, and I decide something. When she comes over tonight, I'm telling her about Alex. The whole sordid story. Lord knows I could use some advice on how to turn things around. If she thinks there's any way I could at least get my friend back.

But for now . . . Alex is waiting. For what, I don't know.

"Do you have, like, two minutes?" I ask her. "Do you mind keeping an eye on Phillip for a sec? He won't move, I promise."

Erin nods and turns her attention to the swing set, granting us some privacy.

I trudge nervously toward Alex. He's not exactly smiling or anything. The shadows under his eyes make him look sort of scary, too.

I stop several feet in front of him.

His eyes flicker toward Erin and the swing set and I wonder if he'll put two and two together and realize I brought Phillip. I hope he doesn't think I did so to make a point, because I didn't, other than that my brother really likes to swing.

"Hey." I try a small smile.

"Hey." He doesn't offer one in return.

I nudge at the ground with my toe. "I guess you're still pissed at me."

"Yep."

His curtness is unexpected and unusual and I inhale as the pain of it hits my chest.

I swallow hard. "I know that. I wouldn't have missed this, though. I wanted to say congratulations in person." Alex still says nothing, so I forge ahead. "Congratulations. You did an amazing thing here."

He allows his eyes to meet mine for only a quick second. There is a trace of warmth but the embers die down quickly. "Thanks."

It's a cold and empty response and I sense that I'm offering too little, too late.

"Is that what you came to say?" Alex asks. "Is there anything else?"

My eyes fly to his and I think I can detect a trace of hope behind the anger, one maybe he wishes I didn't see.

But before I can think about how to begin saying all the things I want to say, he steps away. "If not . . . then I should go. There are a lot of people I need to talk to, and thank." Only one side of his mouth lifts as he offers me a half smile. "Thanks for coming, though." His words aren't authentic, and I guess my presence doesn't count for much at all anymore.

"Bye, Alex," I whisper.

I stare at his retreating back, wondering why the hell it can't be even half as easy with him as it was to repair things with Erin.

But then again, maybe I did a lot more damage to Alex.

Chapter Twelve

That night, after changing into my pajama pants, I find myself pacing back and forth across my room, restless. Even though it was a full day, sleep seems a long way off. I gnaw at my fingernails as I walk.

Erin's not mad at you anymore, I remind myself. *And you did some good deeds for your brother and parents. There's no reason to be this upset.*

But I can't stop picturing the dismissive look on Alex's face before he turned and walked away at the playground, and feel like I have plenty of reason to be upset.

I stare at my car keys on my desk. A moment later, I grab them.

Fibbing to my parents about Erin being in the midst of her latest romantic crisis, I drive across town. Only it's not her house I head toward. I end up parked across the street from the Colby household, fingers poised over the keypad of my phone, ready to dial his number.

But I don't get any farther than that. Earlier at the park, I thought I was silent because I hadn't fully thought through what I want to say to Alex. Now I realize I don't *have* anything to say to him. Not anything worthwhile, at least.

Suddenly I remember thinking one time last month, when Alex said or did something pretty great, that Leighton didn't deserve him.

Do I?

For over a year, I've held on to a memory. Countless times I've wished for a do-over for that moment when I pulled away from him in the supply closet. But that one kiss was a long time ago.

If I consider the person I am now, the choices I've made since then . . . it's hard to believe that Alex would want to kiss that girl anyway.

When I squeeze my eyes shut against this troubling realization, tears seep from the corners. I face the sad realization that if I didn't lose him for good last year, I probably have now. As a potential boyfriend or a friend, it doesn't matter. I'm just sad that I've lost him.

And I decide, for the first time in forever, that I'm *tired* of feeling like the victim of my own life. It's always been so easy to blame Phillip and my parents for anything that's lacking, to use Phillip's disability as an excuse for all the shortcomings in my own life. I've been so comfortable with this attitude, and Alex was right—it's pathetic that I've never managed to step up and reach for something I've wanted if going after it presented any type of risk or put me in an unwanted spotlight.

It's a weak, tired attitude, and as I sit outside his house, accepting that it's indeed *my* attitude, it's hard to feel great about myself. It's hard to believe an apology alone could repair anything between me and the boy inside. I drop the phone onto the passenger seat and head toward home, clueless about how to fix us if I can't find a way to fix me first.

Once a year, my parents need to sign off on my continued participation in the Gifted and Talented program. Monday morning before homeroom, I stop by the small classroom to return the completed paperwork. Mrs. Adamson isn't in the room, so I search for an empty spot on her cluttered desk, hoping she'll see the envelope.

As I push some papers aside, a neon flyer, the one Alex showed me a month and a half ago, catches my eye. It's the announcement for the regional Oracle Society's upcoming high school competition. The date of the contest is little more than a week away. Yet for whatever reason, as I search for the registration deadline, I find myself hoping I haven't missed it.

There it is. If I register by tomorrow, I can still participate.

I let the paper dangle between two fingers and laugh at myself. Am I seriously considering this?

I don't get up in front of crowds of people willingly, and I certainly don't do so by choice.

Plus, the contest is just over a week away! I'm sure that other participants have been working on their speeches—editing, polishing, and practicing in front of the mirror—for weeks, if not months. With one week to go, I'd probably just end up making a fool out of myself.

But I can't stop staring at this year's topic in large, boldface text in the center of the page. "**The Power of Speech.**"

When Alex showed me the flyer before, I thought I had nothing to say on the matter. These days, I feel like I have plenty to say. It's just a matter of, you know, actually *saying* it.

Without further thought, I fold the flyer into a tiny square and shove it into my back pocket as I look around for bystanders, like I'm doing something really shady. Then later, in the library during study hall, I unfold the flyer, log on to the Web site listed at the bottom, and quickly complete the online entry form. I have to provide a teacher's name as a sponsor, and I assume Mrs. Adamson won't mind that I use hers.

When I see the confirmation message pop up on the screen— "Congratulations, Jordyn Michaelson! You are confirmed to participate in the sixteenth annual Southeastern Pennsylvania Oracle Society's high school speech competition"—an unfamiliar thrill goes through me. I'm registered. There's no going back now.

It's sort of liberating, doing something so entirely out of character.

Putting myself out there. Calling attention to myself, my thoughts, and my feelings. On purpose.

I might never tell my parents or friends about the experience, but it's something. It's a first step.

I lean back in the wooden library chair and cross my arms, thinking, focusing my attention on the speech that I now need to get cracking on.

I've been thinking a lot about the concept of speech lately, and it seems like a good place to start.

Remembering the video of Phillip's therapy session, I consider something. To a large capacity, my brother lacks the power of effective speech. I've wasted mine. He can't speak up; I simply choose not to.

We both need a voice, and it's high time I put mine to use, since I can. Even if I'm only ready to share it with a roomful of strangers.

Eight days later, I sit by myself in a crowded auditorium in a Gothic stone building on Villanova University's campus, seriously questioning the sanity behind the belief that I was ready to do *anything* in front of a group of people this large.

The environment is overwhelming in every possible way. The room itself is intimidating, with high ceilings and crystal clear acoustics. I can hear individual voices echoing off the walls, and I feel the cold chill of perspiration under my arms as I imagine how loud my voice will sound in the room when I'm the only one speaking.

I sit near the front right of the crowd and I have a clear view of the panel of judges sitting at a conference table in front of the stage. I know some are college professors, some are local entrepreneurs, and some hold local political office. They have stopwatches, legal pads, and scoring sheets. I'm sure what they don't have is any interest in what I have to say about the concept of speech.

I wipe my clammy palms on the front of my dressiest black pants, which I've paired with loafers and a French blue buttondown shirt. I glance around as I do so, thinking that my attire is another area where I've come up feeling inferior to those around me.

Several of the boys in the crowd are dressed in blazers bearing the insignia from local prep schools, the Hill School and Malvern Preparatory Academy among them. Some of my fellow girls in the group are wearing professional-looking dark suits with heels, as if they're on their way to interviews or board meetings.

And none of them seem to be alone. They sit with teachers or mentors, parents or siblings, and friends from school. They appear both calm and excited, like they're looking forward to this. They make thumbs-up signs as parents' cameras *click-click* away.

I stare down at my lap and fold my hands. When I confided in Mrs. Adamson about the contest, she wanted to come to support me, but I begged her off, insisting this was something I needed to do on my own. My parents think I'm at a study group for history class. I'm probably the only high school junior who uses the excuse of a study group to cover up participation in an oratory contest. This probably seals my fate as a dork with a capital *D*.

At seven o'clock on the dot, the president of the local chapter of the Oracle Society welcomes us and makes some announcements, and then divides us into more manageable groups of eight. Each of us will be allotted ten minutes to present our speeches, with a short intermission halfway through. Lists are handed out and I find my name. I am slated as fifth in line in group one, which will remain in this auditorium to present.

The other groups shuffle off to various rooms, causing a

mass exodus of students, teachers, and parents. The crowd left behind is much smaller, and my utter aloneness in the large room becomes obvious. I see several people turn and assess my solitary presence, which does nothing to calm my nerves. I keep my eyes dead ahead, refusing to look back, because acknowledging anyone in the crowd will only worsen my fears about standing up in front of it.

The lights are dimmed, and the speeches begin. With every participant, I find myself slinking farther and farther down in my seat, berating myself for grasping at the silly belief that I belonged among them. It's not that the content of their speeches is that phenomenal, but, man, are they polished. Their voices never quiver, they smile into the crowd, and they rarely glance down at their notes. They are confident and collected, quite possibly on their way to the debate team at Yale.

I lose count, and suddenly my name is being called. I freeze in my seat and grasp the armrests, certain I can't make myself stand.

Then I take a deep breath, close my eyes, and picture his face. I remember the person I'm here for. I'm not here to win, I'm here to speak. I manage to unpeel my fingers and stand up on shaky legs.

I make my way up the steps without tripping and stand behind the podium, adjusting the microphone. I stare into the distance, relieved that it's impossible to make out individual faces in the crowd with the bright light in my eyes. If anyone is laughing or smirking, I'll be blissfully unaware. I glance down at my notes, just once, and then I start talking.

"Human beings' capacity for and development of speech is a powerful, amazing, almost magical phenomenon. By twelve to eighteen months of age, most humans can easily name objects and people, and describe relationships among them. Most toddlers have learned basic social rituals and greetings. After eighteen months, what is referred to as a 'word explosion' erupts within the young child's brain. A child can speak over one hundred words and understand nearly three times as many. In the next year of life, vocabulary triples. The young human brain not only understands and processes the world it's living in, but uses language to comprehend experiences and relay reactions. By age four, speech is typically intelligible and a child's bank of vocabulary words approaches one thousand. In most cases, speech seems to develop as naturally as breathing, without explicit instruction. In most cases, for most children, the power of speech is taken for granted."

I take a deep breath after spitting out the facts and statistics I committed to memory, apprehensive about moving on to the personal side of this topic.

"When it comes to my fifteen-year-old brother, Phillip, who is autistic, the power of speech cannot be taken for granted." I pause for effect, as some of my fellow competitors have done, and let the words sink in.

"My brother didn't speak his first word until he was almost four years old. By the time most of his peers could use nearly one thousand words, my brother had one. If my parents, an entire team of therapists, and some really exceptional teachers hadn't persistently pushed him, sometimes even provoking frustration or anger, he might never have spoken. Phillip didn't put two words together for another six months, and he wasn't capable of speaking in full sentences until a year after that."

"Almost ten years later, speech still does not come easily to Phillip. Phillip is smart enough to know that he is expected to speak when spoken to. But it's still incredibly tough for Phillip to understand, process, and formulate his own thoughts and feelings. So he compensates in other ways. You may get a Sponge-Bob SquarePants quote when you ask him how his day was, because Phillip has a bank of lines and quotes he's memorized from others to let him off the hook when he is required to reply."

I take another breath, suddenly remember where I am, and feel momentarily panicked. When I exhale, it comes out shakily, and my throat feels like it's constricting. I force myself to remember how panicked Phillip must've felt when that fire alarm went off, and his speech failed him in expressing what the experience felt like inside his brain. I clear my throat and make myself continue.

"But like I said, my brother's a smart boy, and I believe there are a lot of things he'd like people to understand about him, if only the demands of engaging in the world around him weren't so extremely overwhelming. I'd like to take a few minutes tonight to share some of Phillip's challenges, on his behalf."

I tighten my grasp on the outside edges of the podium, sincerely hoping I will do his experience justice, that I can come even remotely close to capturing it.

"Most of us have a choice regarding the challenges we take on. I made the choice to stand up in front of all of you tonight, even though it's something that does not come naturally to me, and my palms are so sweaty that they're sliding right off this podium." I manage a smile for the crowd. "But ultimately, I had some level of control—I could choose to show up and face this challenge, or I could choose to skip out and avoid it.

"Largely, Phillip does not have this choice, because so many tiny aspects of life are painful to him. For most of us, a trip to the mall at this time of the year is unpleasant because of crowded parking lots and the length of the line at Starbucks. For Phillip, it's downright hostile. His hearing is so acute it sounds like ten thousand people are talking around him at once rather than ten or twenty. Registers beep, babies scream, and the canned music is a persistent swarm of bees in his ears. He might try to block some of it out, but it's hard, what with how the fluorescent lighting burns his eyes, preventing him from focusing, and everything and everybody passing in his peripheral vision moves too fast to be processed.

"The assault on his senses comes from every angle. My brother probably knows that the man in front of us on the escalator didn't shower that day and that the cashier smoked a cigarette on her drive to work. The seasoned ground beef in the vats at Taco Bell is nauseating, and he can detect it a corridor away. A janitor used a cleaning solution with ammonia to mop the night before, and it still burns Phillip's nostrils.

"Everything around him is moving and swirling and assaulting his brain, which can't separate and process the input, and ends up in overload mode. The sounds give him a headache, the sights compel him to close his eyes, and the smells drive him to the brink of vomiting." I stare into the faceless crowd. "Put yourself in his shoes and imagine how badly you'd want to escape. I'd imagine you'd do whatever it takes to get out of there.

"One time I got a migraine when I was at the grocery store with my mother," I relay to the crowd. "I started seeing spots, and my hands were shaking. I was scared I was going to throw up. I said, 'Mom, I need to go home; I don't feel well,' and we left within minutes. Now imagine you are Phillip, who is similarly incapacitated from everyday experiences, but also lacks the words to express how he feels like he is trapped within a war zone.

"What would you do?" I wonder aloud. "What would you do to let someone know? How would you communicate without the power of speech?"

My questions hang in the open air for a moment before I continue.

"Well, you might hit, for one. You might fall to the ground. You might scream. You might cry like a child thirteen years younger than your chronological age. Because without the power of speech, how do you let someone know you're hurting?

"Phillip does all these things, several times a week. And because they're the only tools he has to communicate with, Phillip's bizarre behaviors, rather than his thoughts, come to define him. I've heard my brother called weird. Crazy. Retarded. Psycho. Dangerous." I smile wryly. "It's sad that 'weird' is the least offensive on the list. But because Phillip can't speak well, he is defined narrowly—he is defined by his autism.

"I play field hockey," I inform the crowd. "Specifically, I'm a midfielder. That's one part of who I am, one thing I do. Like me, Phillip is more than just one thing. Phillip has a range of thoughts, feelings, talents, and preferences. He is a whiz at math and he outperformed me on the PSATs. His favorite color is green. He loves to swing. He'll do almost anything to get you to share your pretzel sticks with him. His favorite movie is *Dirty Rotten Scoundrels*. Phillip has a sense of humor." My throat tightens on the next line. "And when he shares it with you, he has a smile that will melt your heart. Like all of us, I believe Phillip just wants to be loved unconditionally, for who he is, because he can't really change that. Phillip's autism is a part of who he is, and I don't deny that it's a big part. But it's never going to be all that he is. He should be loved for all that he is."

Something I've failed at miserably so far, I realize. I've done worse than reduce Phillip to a robot; I've reduced him to a problem.

Even though I know I have several minutes left on the clock, I find myself wishing the timekeeper would sound the warning bell. I wish I didn't have to finish my speech, because I'm scared I'm not going to be able to. I'm scared my power of speech might fail me in my attempt to reveal what's in my heart. But no bell sounds to rescue me, and I push on.

"As Phillip's older sister, I've had plenty of opportunities to share the things I've shared tonight with the rest of the world. With kids at school. With teachers who have training but still lack full understanding. With members of the community. With anyone who can't even begin to understand what life is like for Phillip, that it's a miracle of strength that he gets out of bed and faces the outside world each and every day. Before today, I've barely said a word."

I lift my chin. "I stand here tonight and tell you it is a shameful regret, because just recently I realized something. Phillip *can't* speak up, and I have *chosen* not to. It is disrespectful to him that

I squander my power of speech, that I have wasted opportunities to advocate for, protect, defend, and help my brother. Or even just to call him my brother.

"There have always been plenty of reasons to keep quiet," I admit. "Phillip can be embarrassing at times. Because I've seen how often people reduce Phillip to his disability, I worry about being reduced in the same way, as his sister and nothing else. I hate the idea of being seen as weird, crazy, or psycho by association. I kept my distance because it seemed easier at the time, but I've started to learn that might not be the case." I find myself thinking of Erin . . . and Alex. "The distance has cost me and it has cost my brother."

I hang my head and stare at the wood grain of the podium platform, trying to will away the tears I worry about forming in front of my eyes. "There's another reason why I think I've kept my distance from Phillip. Autism, his limited speech . . . they don't just keep Phillip trapped inside another world, apart from us. Somehow, in a way I haven't fully come to understand yet, his autism keeps us locked away from him, too. It's hard to give my heart to my brother. It's really hard to say the words *I love you* when you know you'll likely never hear them back."

I picture my brother, the one who's never said the words, the one who's never given me a hug. I remember the baby picture from the hospital, the brother I'd longed for that never really came home. It's pretty futile to fight the tears, and I stop trying. "Sometimes, that idea just hurts too much, and you end up keeping your distance for a whole other reason. You develop a terrible habit of doing so. The idea of saying 'I love you' starts to seem scary."

I feel two tears tumble gently onto my cheeks, but I don't

brush at them, hoping no one will notice. I give myself a long pause, making sure my voice is steady before attempting to finish.

"Tonight, with both a microphone and a crowd in front of me, I am using my power of speech to say the words out loud. I love you, Phillip, and I'm proud of you. You are ten times stronger than I'll ever be. You are not weird, crazy, retarded, or psycho. You are strong, brave, funny, and resilient. I would like to be as strong and brave as you are, and today is my first step." My voice cracks, but I'm past the point of caring. "I love you, and tonight, for you, I take that feeling beyond the privacy of our home or the quiet confines of my heart. I'm going to work on loving you out loud. I'm going to work on living out loud."

My chin shakes, my eyes are brimming, and my voice is weak. But I finish my speech. "I have the power of speech. And in your honor, I refuse to take it for granted anymore."

I dash down the steps. I grab my purse from my seat and hurry out of the auditorium, leaving the silence of the crowd behind me.

I never had any plans to stay for the results and I don't really care to hear my score. A victory is not something I wished for in the first place.

I just wish he could have been here to hear me say it. I wish he was capable of understanding not just my words, but the emotion behind them. I want Phillip to know, in my heart, he is more than an inconvenience or an embarrassment. He is my brother. And that idea isn't scary anymore.

Chapter Thirteen

On Tuesday night, I was too emotionally spent by the end of my speech to even think about how it was received. But, as someone who's amassed all those ribbons, certificates, and awards my mother has stockpiled, I should've known my underlying high-achieving tendencies would reveal themselves. Curiosity gets the better of me, and the next morning before school, I log on to the contest's Web site.

The results are posted. I didn't win first prize, or place as first or second runner-up. But I'm a bit flabbergasted to find that out of twenty-six participants, my name is among the three listed as honorable mentions.

A photo of the winners accompanies the list. I recognize several of those boys in the prep school blazers wearing medals on striped ribbons around their necks. The honorable mention winners are among them, holding small winner's cups.

I wonder if my recognition was attributed to the content of my speech or my presentation of it, and I hope it's a little bit of both. I feel the slightest twinge of regret that I didn't make myself stay. On one hand, I accomplished what I set out to achieve—I proved myself to myself, even if I haven't yet proved myself to the people I care about. On the other hand, it would've been sort of nice to have the moment captured on film. So I could remember that sometimes it pays off to speak up.

Maybe the contest organizers will mail me my trophy or something. I'll put it away but I'll be able to look at it from time to time. And that will be the end of the oratory contest.

Except, as it turns out, that's not the end of it. Not at all.

When I walk into independent study that afternoon, Mrs. Adamson asks to see me in the hallway. She grabs a small blue gift bag off her desk, and I follow her, trying to ignore the feel of Alex's curious stare on my back.

Once we're alone, she smiles brightly and hands me the bag. "Congratulations, Jordyn!"

I peek inside the bag. There sits my trophy.

There's a handwritten note alongside it.

I really wish you had stayed to receive the recognition you deserved for such an important, heartfelt speech. I felt responsible for making sure you received this.

It is signed "Judith Devereux, Professor of Social Psychology, Villanova University."

I remember one of the female judges, sitting at the end of the panel, in a wheelchair. My instincts tell me it was Judith.

I beam a little bit inside, thrilled at this type of acknowledgment. From a professor! At a real university!

"The secretary said someone dropped it off this morning," Mrs. Adamson tells me. "She said the woman passes the school on her way into work. Since I was listed as your sponsoring teacher, it made its way to me. I was so excited to see your trophy in that bag. What an accomplishment."

I blush and mumble a thank-you, twisting the handles of the bag in my hands.

Then Mrs. Adamson glances back toward the classroom. "That being said, it's pretty obvious that you aren't particularly comfortable sharing about this experience." She points toward a recognition bulletin board on the wall where she has posted noteworthy student achievements. The newspaper article about Alex's playground is among them. "I would love to give you the recognition you deserve, but . . ."

She looks at me expectantly, awaiting an explanation.

I look at the floor. "It was a really personal thing."

I hope she doesn't press.

Luckily, Mrs. Adamson has always been kind and understanding, and she lets the subject drop. But first she pulls a slim, square case from behind her back. "She sent this, too." I reach out and accept the DVD she offers me. "Just know I'd love to watch it someday if you ever change your mind." She chuckles. "I'm proud of you, that's for sure, even if I can't fully see why."

I hastily shove the DVD into the bag with the trophy and Professor Devereux's note. "I know it doesn't make sense that such a public thing is actually so private and personal, but . . . it just is."

She puts a hand on my shoulder. "It's your experience. You don't have to explain yourself to me."

We return to the classroom without further discussion. Alex continues to stare as I shove the blue bag as quickly as humanly possible into my book bag.

When I sit back up . . . he's still looking at me.

Alex hasn't looked at me, not really, since he walked away from me at the playground over a week ago. But now he's looking at me again and he looks sad. His face is constricted and his lips are parted, like he has something to say, sitting right there on the tip of his tongue.

But this time around, it's Alex who remains speechless. He gives me one last pained look before dropping his head and returning to his work.

That night, I situate the trophy in my bottom desk drawer on top of the note. I plan to put the DVD in there, too.

Funny thing, though, once the DVD's in my possession. It sort of burns a proverbial hole in my pocket. I can't bring myself to tuck it away with the other mementos from the night.

Not that I want to watch it. *God.* I cringe at the very idea of seeing myself on our forty-two-inch flat-screen, especially toward the end of my speech, when my tears got the better of me.

But I keep thinking of why my mom said she wanted to take Phillip to the Sparkle Ball, how she wanted the world to give Phillip even a sliver of the recognition it gave me. I feel like I have, in some small way, given him that public recognition. I'd trounced the idea of the Sparkle Ball, something I still feel guilty about. I turn the DVD case over and over in my hands. But maybe . . .

The next morning, I act quickly, without further thought. I slip the DVD into her purse on my way out the door. I don't leave any explanation. She'll figure it out.

Hours later, when I walk in the door after practice, it's obvious that she has.

She rises from the couch, eyes red. "Come here," she demands, as she walks toward me and engulfs me in a crushing hug. "I've never been more proud of you in my whole life," she whispers into my ear.

My body turns rigid in her grasp, uncomfortable. This sort of praise . . . it's the last thing I wanted.

She pulls back but keeps her grasp on my arms, jiggling them. "Why on earth didn't you *tell* us, though? I would've given anything to be there. To hear you. And support you! My God, what it must've taken, to get up on that stage . . ."

"I didn't want to say anything ahead of time," I lie. "I was scared I might not go through with it and then there'd be more people to embarrass myself in front of." I smile wanly, hoping she buys it.

The lie is the best I can offer, because I don't want to offend her with the truth. I wasn't doing it to gain credit or to make amends, either. I wasn't doing it for her or my father. It was something I needed to do for myself, and for Phillip. That moment that I stood up there and said those words aloud . . . I wanted it to be pure.

"Well, I am just really, really glad you decided to share it with me, that I got to see it in some capacity. Maybe Dad can watch it, too?" Her voice is hopeful. "He should be home any minute."

I nod and turn toward the stairs. I know sharing was the right thing to do, but I can't stand here in the glow of her praise any longer. I never meant for this to be about me.

But before my foot hits the bottom step, my mom's words stop me dead in my tracks.

"You were so very right, Jordyn," she says quietly, behind me. "It's really hard to love him sometimes, isn't it?"

I whirl around, surprised at her blunt admission.

She stares at the floor, as if ashamed. "There's not a single day that passes when I don't *know* that I love your brother," she corrects herself. "But knowing it and feeling it are two different things. And some days . . . for all those reasons you said, it's not always easy to feel it. It hurts too much."

Now she looks up at me and frowns. "I don't think I ever could have said that out loud before today, before watching this." She lifts the DVD in her hand. "It was very brave of you, speaking the truth like that, saying the things no one wants to think or feel."

Then my mother stares at me for a very long time, appraising the person she sees before her, her lips pressed into a thin line, head tilted to the side.

"You were forced to become independent at a very young age," she muses. She tilts her head to the other side, and considers me some more. "I always thought that was a good thing. But in this video, I think for the first time, I saw you being brave."

Something catches in my chest. No one's ever called me brave before.

She straightens up and a contented smile lingers on her face. "I like brave. It's a good look on you."

I can't keep the smile off my face, because this praise, I like. This praise, I earned. This praise *is* about me. "Thanks, Mom."

Then the smile slowly slides off her face and her hands twitch nervously at her sides. "Speaking of being brave . . ." She tugs at her earring and clears her throat. "I never told you that I went ahead and accepted the invitation to the Sparkle Ball. It's on Saturday night."

"Okay."

I'm not going to criticize her decision again, it's hers to make.

Then I realize she's staring at me hopefully. "The committee sent us six tickets. . . ."

I get where she's going and I groan audibly.

"Phillip's not the only person who overcomes his autism," she continues in a rush. "We overcome it every day, all of us. I think we should *all* be recognized, to be perfectly honest."

I push my hair off my forehead and exhale mightily. "Mom . . . it's going to be such a disaster."

"Can it be worse than anything else we've ever experienced with Phillip?"

Before I can reply that yes, it can, because there will be *video cameras* capturing it on film, she has grabbed her purse and is riffling through her wallet. She digs out her American Express card and thrusts it at me. "You can get a new dress. You don't even have to take me shopping with you. Take Erin. Pick out whatever you want."

I raise my eyebrows at the card in my hand. She is breaking all her rules. I've never been allowed to go formal dress shopping without her, and every Spring Fling and Fall Homecoming Frolic outfit has been Mom-approved first.

"You're really desperate, huh?"

"I meant what I said earlier. I've never been more proud of you. I want to celebrate *both* my children. You're a part of his success. You've given a lot, even before you said it out loud." She rolls her eyes and sighs. "All those nights when your only dinner was cheddar popcorn . . ."

I laugh, because I never would have thought she remembered. But she does.

Then I palm the card, sigh, and roll my eyes. "I guess I'll think about it."

But I'm already thinking that my answer is yes.

I feel like I've changed a lot since my mom initially told me about the ball. I've endured a lot, too. I flip the credit card over in my hands, frowning at it, thinking of what's been lost. I have nothing to lose anymore by attending the ball and I know very well that other experiences are much more painful.

I end up inviting both Erin and Tanu to go last-minute dress shopping with me on Friday night.

Tanu has plans, but Erin accepts quickly. I'm very happy to have her along. King of Prussia Mall is the largest on the East Coast, and the first week of November, its more than four *hundred* stores are already crowded with overeager Christmas shoppers. Erin helps me stay focused.

We scan the dress selections at Bloomingdale's, Macy's, and Lord & Taylor before deciding on one from Nordstrom. Erin picks it out—a dark pink strapless dress with a short, flouncy skirt. I'm glad my mother is not along, because she definitely would have raised an eyebrow. Erin assures me that short dresses are considered "ball" appropriate these days, and that its shiny gem tone is *the* shade this fall.

I take her word for it, buy the dress, and treat her to a giant monster cookie in the café on the third floor of the department store.

"So do you know where Tanu is tonight?" I ask, after taking a bite of my oatmeal raisin cookie and a sip of ice-cold milk. "I swear she blushed when she said she was busy. Then she dashed off. So not like her."

Erin giggles. "Yep. I do know. She's going to the movies. With Kevin Novak."

I know the kind, if slightly bookish, sophomore from the Gifted and Talented classroom. "Well, good for her. Why is she embarrassed?"

"Who the hell knows?" Erin shrugs, then frowns. "At least she has someone to go out with."

"Speaking of . . ." She continues a minute later, as she picks at an M&M on her cookie and glances at me from the corner of her eye, ". . . Do you get to take a date to the ball?"

The thought has never crossed my mind. We have an extra ticket, because we were given six. That's a ticket for everyone in my family, and Terry Roth, who nominated Phillip, plans to meet us there. But her husband can't go, so as it stands . . . there's an extra ticket. One that I have absolutely no use for.

"Who would I ask? Especially with less than twenty-four hours' notice?"

Erin tilts her head and gives me a Look.

I drop my head and stare at my cookie crumbs. "Nothing's changed since last week, Erin," I mumble. "He's not really even speaking to me."

"Well, have you spoken to *him*?"

"No."

"From what you told me, he said plenty, Jordyn." She shakes her head. "I mean, a boy delivers a speech like *that* . . . you talk to him, you idiot!"

My head snaps up in surprise. "Erin!"

"I'm just saying, he already put it on the line for you. Isn't it time you did the same, if you care at all?"

I swish the milk around in my glass. "He doesn't seem to be in a very forgiving mood." I roll my eyes. "And Lord knows Leighton sure as hell isn't, either." I meet her eyes, pleading, thinking she of all people will understand the powerful girl code at play here. And she, more than anyone else, would hate to have Leighton pissed off at her. "She's out to ruin my life now." I close my eyes and wince, thinking about what she's already accomplished. "My car was covered in shaving cream this morning, that's why I was late." I'd hurried to clean it off before my parents saw because I couldn't even think about how I'd explain it to them. "And some girl I've never even spoken to called me a slut in the bathroom." I shake my head. "Last week, she probably didn't even know my name. This week I'm a slut."

But Erin surprises me. "Season's over next week, so you won't be seeing her that much anymore," she reminds me. "And she may have all her friends riled up right now, but ultimately? They'll move on to something or someone else." She lifts and lowers her shoulders once. "She has to know she's going to end up looking pathetic if she can't let Alex go and continues to make a fool of herself over the guy who dumped her. A *younger* guy who dumped her. Leighton hates to lose, but even more than that, she hates acknowledging defeat," she finishes sagely. "I think she'll move on faster than you think."

When I don't answer, she asks me a final, quiet question. "Which one of them do you care about more?"

It's such an obvious answer, and one I wish I'd been ready to answer when Alex had unloaded his feelings on me in the parking lot. I wish I'd been prepared to take everything he'd offered me.

I sigh. "It might be too late, though. I'm pretty sure Alex has written me off."

"Then what do you have to lose?" Erin sits up straight and crumples her napkin. "Ask him. Why not? At least you tried then." Her eyes get all distant and misty. "Ask him. If he says yes . . . it'll be so romantic!"

"It's not a movie, Erin. He's *not* going to say yes. Anyway," I change the subject, "you'll definitely come help me with my hair, right?"

The next night, at six thirty, I watch through the window as the rented limo pulls up in front of our house. My family is already outside waiting. I let the curtain fall, glance at the clock a final time, heart heavy, and go join them.

I can't shake the sadness hanging over me, but it's impossible not to smile when I see Phillip outside in his tux. My mom couldn't cajole him into letting her comb his hair, and it's standing straight up on one side, but he still looks really nice. We had to buy the shirt so my mother could cut all the tags out and patch over them, since they drive Phillip crazy, but I guess it's worth it. Phillip may never go to a prom and who knows if he'll ever marry. He may never wear a tux again, but it's something worth seeing.

When Phillip sees me walking toward the sidewalk, he starts up again right away.

"We must save the princess!" he says urgently. "We must save the princess!"

His voice is robotic as he quotes a line from one Super Mario game or another, but I decide to take his words as a compliment, anyway. I sort of feel like a princess. The dress totally works, once I paired it with strappy silver sandals, long dangly jeweled earrings, and a gunmetal-gray clutch I borrowed from Erin. When she was over earlier, she arranged my hair into a messy chignon with lots of loose pieces around my face. I barely recognized myself in the mirror when she was finished.

"Smile!" she prompted me. "You look totally hot!"

I managed a halfhearted smile in the mirror, but there was nothing to turn it real. I glanced at my phone a final time, but the little envelope on the faceplate alerting me to new mail never blinked. Alex didn't respond. Alex isn't coming.

Friday night after my shopping trip with Erin, I e-mailed him. Bolstered by Erin's speech and remembering what my mother had said—*I like brave. It's a good look on you*"—I sent a short message, not wanting to put him on the spot with a phone call or late-night personal visit. I explained to him that I'd really like a chance to talk and that I would really like to introduce my family to him if he was willing to give me another shot at friendship. In a last-minute burst of courage, I invited him to join us for the ball.

Now the e-mail just seems silly and I wish I'd never sent it.

I looked at my phone all morning, while pretending to do my homework and clean my room. I ran my finger over the screen a million times while Erin was over helping me get ready. She seemed surprised he hadn't responded, but I couldn't be.

"Alex gave me a lot of chances," I mumbled, staring down at the dark phone on my lap. "I told you, he's done."

Yet I guess I didn't totally believe it, not really, until this very moment. It's six thirty, Alex has not shown up, and it's time to go. I'm the last person to climb into the limo, my pathetically hopeful eyes sweeping the empty street a final time. His car is not driving down it.

There is a feeling of vastness in my stomach, an ocean of unshed tears. It is only in this moment that I accept the truth of how badly I wanted things to turn out differently. And this truth brings an awful sadness I must battle back.

I lower my head, plaster on a smile for my mother, and climb into the car.

Once we're on our way and I know there's no chance of the night turning out differently, I try to forget about the e-mail and my silly fantasies about what could've been. It's kind of fun riding in a limo, and Phillip seems to get a kick out of it. My father produces a bottle of sparkling grape juice and we use the champagne glasses from the limo's bar to toast the evening.

At first, when we pull up in front of the Four Seasons, my heart sinks to the pit of my stomach. I lower the window and take it all in—there's an actual red carpet, the news reporters with microphones and cameras, the cheering, glittering crowd . . . the overall sense of noise, color, and chaos.

Phillip's going to go batshit crazy. I know it.

But then a representative from the Happiness Circuit approaches our car and calmly and quietly explains there is a separate, private red carpet entrance around the block for kids who are shy or have sensory issues. He directs our driver, and a moment later, I feel a huge sense of relief as I assess the private entrance. It still boasts a red carpet, but there is only a single photographer to capture the arrivals and a much smaller, quieter crowd.

Phillip is given his headphones and emerges from the car with little prodding. The crowd on the second red carpet has clearly been instructed not to clap, and instead, the various community members and Happiness Circuit representatives hold up signs—WE'RE PROUD OF YOUR ACCOMPLISHMENTS!, CHEERS TO YOU!, and ENJOY YOUR SPECIAL NIGHT!

Still, Phillip is on a mission to get past the crowd, and despite my mom's instructions for him to slow down and pose for the camera, he continues on his course.

At the last minute, I call his name, and when he turns to me, I pull out my secret weapon. From my clutch, I retrieve a small cardboard cutout of SpongeBob, which I'd stapled to a Popsicle stick. I wave it back and forth in front of my face, knowing it will produce a smile.

There it is! I hear the click of the camera in the nick of time, and I smile along with him in satisfaction. My mom deserves one good picture for her memory box, and I'd suspected it would take some preplanning to guarantee that for her.

She looks over her shoulder, blinking back tears as she throws me a grateful smile before chasing after Phillip into the ballroom.

Heavy heart aside, I'm feeling pretty good about things as I walk down the red carpet. Phillip has successfully entered the Sparkle Ball. My family is in good spirits. I'm wearing a beautiful dress and it's time for a party.

But I've taken only three steps when I catch sight of something—*someone*—just before the entrance that makes me stop dead in my tracks. It would be easy for him to blend in to the background, dressed as he is, like all the other men in the crowd, in a tuxedo.

But to me, it would be impossible for him not to stand out.

He looks more handsome than I've ever seen him—mature, clean-cut, and stunning.

The look on his face is inscrutable and his eyes are dark.

Yet he is here.

Alex is here.

Chapter Fourteen

There's a feeling when you wake from a particularly exceptional dream, a mixture of sadness, loss, and disbelief. Then there are those seconds just prior, when you're awake but still able to hold on to the images from the night, a few seconds of fleeting, too-good-to-be-true happiness.

I have that second feeling as I stand at the end of a red carpet, staring at Alex.

He is too good to be true, a mirage that will surely vanish into thin air if I stand here and continue to stare.

Except Alex doesn't vanish. Alex starts walking toward me.

I am frozen, dumbfounded. "What are you doing here?"

He grimaces at my less-than-polite greeting, but I think I see a trace of the dimple in his cheek. "My mistake." Alex cocks an eyebrow. "I was under the impression that I was invited."

"Oh. Um. Right."

I fiddle with my clutch, snapping and unsnapping the clasp.

I am really botching this.

But it's hard to look at him, as handsome and regal as he looks.

"Anyway, I thought you still might be looking for a date."

At the word *date*, Alex coughs once and brings his fist to his mouth to cover it up. I realize he is nervous, which is endearing and sort of unbelievable at the same time. What on earth does he have to be nervous about?

"If not a date . . . well, at least a friend," he clarifies.

I force myself to make eye contact with him. "You've been really pissed at me. I didn't think that had changed."

But Alex looks away, staring at the space over my shoulder, and shoves his hands into the pockets of his tuxedo pants. I can't help but admire his profile, his clean-shaven jaw and the softness of his lips.

"I haven't been pissed for a few days now."

Really? What had changed? He hadn't even spoken to me.

"Why not?"

He continues to evade my eyes and squares his jaw. "I saw something that changed my mind. I saw a speech."

I inhale suddenly, with surprise. *What?*

Had Mrs. Adamson made a copy of the DVD? Had she been entirely careless and just left it lying around? Or had she actively made a point of sharing my most private moment with my classmates?

I tighten my grasp on my bag. "How did you get the DVD?"

Alex shakes his head, still staring into the distance. "I didn't see any DVD," he answers. Only then does he bring his gaze to mine. "I was there."

My heart stops in my chest. Again . . . *what?*

I am too gobsmacked to formulate the obvious question.

"I wasn't trying to snoop," he explains. "But . . . Mrs. Adamson printed out your registration form. It was sitting in the printer when I went to pick up my English assignment."

His head is lowered, his brows drawn. "I should have asked you before coming, but . . . we weren't exactly on speaking terms. And I just had to see . . . I wanted to know what you would say when you thought people you knew weren't listening."

I'm still a few steps behind him, trying to wrap my head around all of this. How did I possibly miss Alex? How had his presence gone unnoticed?

Then I remember the night of the contest, my staunch refusal to turn around and assess the intimidating crowd and the glaring lights that impeded my vision.

The way I made a mad dash from the room when I finished my speech.

"I would have told you I was there, but you ran away before I could." Alex pauses, swallowing hard, his Adam's apple nervously pressing against his neck. "Then I was too . . ." His voice falls off, even as he tries a second time to spit his words out. "Then I was too . . ."

His unfinished sentence hangs in the air for an eternity.

"Too what?"

Alex's eyes don't waver as he looks at me. His voice is almost harsh. "I was too *sad*, Jordyn, okay? I was too sad." He closes his eyes for a second, full lashes beating against the top of his cheeks. "You were so mature and so brave." His eyes fly open. "You were so real, and more than ever, I wished . . . I wished things were different."

Alex tries to smile, and cracks his knuckles once, but his attempts at casualness don't work. "I've been kind of miserable since then," he admits, letting out an awkward chuckle. "So when you e-mailed me, I knew something had to change." He gives me a goofy smile. "So I decided to show up. So we could go back to being friends, or whatever."

For the second time in my life, Alex Colby stands in front of me, conceding to the idea of friendship.

No. Freakin'. Way.

Not this time.

It's now or never, the moment I've thought about nearly a million times since I stood in that rainy parking lot, weak and pathetic and *silent*.

If I managed to share my most private emotions with a crowd of strangers, then I have to be able to share them with the person I care about the most.

So I don't laugh along with him. We could turn this into a joke, or we could get serious.

There's a lot at risk. My social survival at school. Life as I know it, in general.

My heart.

When I delivered my speech, I learned the reward was sometimes worth the risk. I hope to God giving Alex my heart is worth the risk, too.

"I've been miserable, too," I admit. "I've been miserable way longer than a few days."

Alex looks pained and his hand reaches toward mine, just barely covering it.

"Everything you put out there in the parking lot . . ." I take a final deep breath and forge ahead. "I want it. I want all those things, Alex. I want you."

His hand tightens ever so slightly over mine.

"It might be hard. Leighton will likely make my life a living hell. She'll have an entire group of people out to get me. They'll keep saying awful things about me—and my brother, well, she's *already* called him every name in the book."

Alex's eyes darken and he opens his mouth to say something, but I put a hand up to stop him. "But I'm done trying to protect myself from the hurt that may or may not come." I swallow hard and stare at my feet. "Turns out trying to do so causes a way worse kind of pain. And I don't want to hurt like that anymore. I don't want to push you away."

Alex takes one step closer. His arms tighten around me, and he pulls me to his chest. "I wouldn't let you anyway," he whispers. He rests his chin atop my head and I hear and feel him sigh with relief against me. Alex's hands glide over my shoulders, and linger in a path down my back. Then he tightens his grasp again, holding me close for an eternity, like he never wants to let me go.

The warmth of his body melts into mine. I feel the firmness of his thighs, the strength of his chest, where his heart is pounding in a rapid flutter.

Since last summer, Alex has thrown his arm around my shoulder a million times. He has given me countless silly fist bumps. He has even playfully ruffled my hair.

But Alex hasn't hugged me, not like this.

I haven't had physical contact with Alex in so long and I am suddenly, painfully aware of exactly how badly I've been craving it.

I am back in that closet at the tennis club, remembering exactly how perfect kissing Alex felt. I'd like to do it again.

Except, I suddenly remember, we are standing on a red carpet. There are TV cameras nearby. And my father is hovering in the entranceway. Probably best to stick with a hug.

I allow myself a minute, then take a step back. I nod my head in the direction of the ballroom and my dad scurries inside, like he *wasn't* staring. The DJ is gearing up inside and I see flashing lights from the dance floor.

I don't let go of his hand, though. It is warm and strong and perfect, especially when he intertwines his fingers with mine.

"So, you want to go check out the party?"

Alex smiles at me, his first real, huge smile since . . . this. Since just about forever, it feels like. "Might as well," he answers. He tugs at his lapels and a familiar teasing light enters his eyes. "Be a shame to waste this much dapper . . ."

I swat his chest with my clutch, happy and relieved that Alex is still Alex, even now that Alex is mine.

We enter the hotel and I leave my wrap in the coat closet before we join the party.

Inside the main ballroom, it's a black-tie carnival. In addition to the buffet, there is an entire dessert room, with chocolate fountains, funnel cake fries, and even cotton candy. There are games, raffles, and face painting. The DJ is playing loud, cheesy music, and the younger kids never leave the dance floor, some trying to do their best to follow along with the Cha Cha Slide and Chicken Dance in wheelchairs or with legs in braces.

Their faces are happy, washed with color and flashing lights, as they enjoy their stint as celebrities. One night where they shine instead of standing out.

Phillip seems pretty happy, too, once he discovers the video-game room sponsored by Nintendo.

I introduce Alex to my parents. Their eyes fly to our hands, which are still linked. They've never seen me with a boy, not one that I'm introducing as mine. My mom's lips twitch a bit as she tries to keep her smile at bay. My father pales slightly.

Then I introduce Alex to Phillip. Alex is as kind, compassionate, and genuine as I'd expect him to be.

Phillip is as . . . well, Phillip as I'd expect him to be. And that's okay. I'm not bothered. I'm not bothered at all.

After Alex and I eat, I allow him to coerce me onto the dance floor for more silly selections, like the Cupid Shuffle and some other group dance I'd never bothered to learn.

I roll my eyes at Alex as I agree to join him. "I guess so. As long as we're just being ironic."

"Get over yourself, Michaelson." Alex wraps his arms around me as he nudges me toward the dance floor. "This is fun and you know it."

For the second time that night I consider how much I'd really like this boy to kiss me.

It's a pretty great night, and by the time it's over, I can hardly remember my state of mind when I told my mom what an absolutely awful idea the Sparkle Ball was. We have so much fun, Alex and I, competing against each other at the carnival games and stuffing our faces with funnel cake fries dripping with powdered sugar.

Alex came down on the train and my parents invite him to ride home in the limo with us. So just before the ball ends at eleven o'clock, he walks me to the coat closet to collect my wrap. The attendant has left for the evening, and before we walk inside to find my wrap, Alex's head whips back and forth across the empty lobby. He licks his lips once and then pulls me hurriedly inside.

We are bathed in near darkness and I find myself following Alex's lead until my back is pressed against a soft wall of wool, tweed, and something that feels a lot like fur.

Alex's hands find my hips. My throat dries up at once and my heart takes off like a freight train, knowing the moment is here, knowing I'll no longer just be *thinking* about kissing Alex. I'll actually be kissing Alex.

The irony of it all dawns, and I start running my mouth, nervous. "What is it with you and closets?" I croak.

Alex lowers his lips to my ear and I can hear him smirking in the darkness. "Truth be told, I hate closets."

His mouth grazes my earlobe, sending an onslaught of chills down my spine. His fingertips dance over my hip bones. "I have a conditioned fear of closets, actually." Alex raises his head, finding the other side of my neck with his lips. He plants the smallest of kisses there and I hear my breath vibrating in the air between us. "One time, this girl completely crushed me inside a closet."

He brushes his forehead back and forth across mine, and we

are sharing the same breath now, and I know within a matter of seconds, Alex will kiss me.

Only I don't want him to because it's time for me to make a move. It's time for me to *finally* make a move.

My hands find his jaw in the darkness. "This girl has regretted that moment a million times over," I whisper. "This girl is really sorry."

Then I bring his face all the way to mine. I kiss Alex.

It is not the intense, all-consuming kiss from last summer. It is a soft spark rather than a raging fire, all gentle lips, traces of powdered sugar, and soft hands. It's perfection.

Then Alex rests his forehead on my shoulder. "The thing that broke my heart about your speech," he begins, "was that part where you said how hard it is to say 'I love you' knowing that you'll never hear it back. . . ."

He brushes the hair back from my face, continuing to whisper to me. His hands are trembling. "You should know . . . you should know . . ."

It is one more thing I don't want to make him do first.

"Just wait a minute," I whisper.

I think how he was brave enough to confront me in the parking lot, how honest he was, how he shared with me all the things he saw in me last summer.

I lace my fingers back through his and hold his hands against my heart. "I noticed you, too, you know. Last summer. I saw you, too. I remember the very first second I laid eyes on you, how your smile was pure sunshine and how you'd share it with anyone." I let go of his hands and trace his lips with my fingers, feeling them part softly at my touch.

"I noticed how kind your heart was. And I knew at once how rare, and special, and good you were." My hand slips down to his chest, inside his lapel, and I actually *feel* his heart pounding in response to my words.

Tears fill my throat, and they are a mixture of happy and sad, regret and hope. "I remember falling in love with my best friend." I pull his head closer to mine. I whisper into his ear. "I've never stopped. I loved you right away and I've never stopped."

His response is an exhalation of relief and joy. "I love you, too, Jordyn. Thank you for *finally* letting me say it out loud."

We find each other again in the darkness.

Our second kiss is the one I remember, the one I've longed for for over a year. It is starched cotton crushed against taffeta, my hands running over the planes of his strong back as I claim his body with no fear of the consequences. It is heartbeat matching heartbeat, as they both take off, ignited by the fire that sparks between us. We fumble in our attempts to get close enough, determined to close the distance that never should have existed in the first place.

My life might never be perfect, but I'm really glad it's mine. I happen to really like my life now, too much to care about what anyone else has to say about it. I like it enough to fight for it.

Holding Alex's hand, I pull him out of the dark room, ready to take on the world. Together.

Acknowledgments

Jean Feiwel and Holly West, I will never be able to fully convey my gratitude. I understand there is great happiness in making "the call," and I can only tell you, it increases exponentially at the receiving end. Thank you for giving me this opportunity when the Swoon imprint was still young, and for your faith and support along the way. Zoey Peresman, I'm extremely grateful for your enthusiasm and contributions to this project. Allison Verost, thank you—as promised. A good margarita is never forgotten. To the rest of the Swoon team, thank you for your warmth and excitement about my story, for whipping it into shape and making it look pretty. I'm honored to be associated with such an innovative, energetic, and creative team.

Capturing emotions in words is a passion of mine, and I am so thankful for this opportunity to have a voice. I want to acknowledge all the students I've met who struggle to understand the world of words around them and convey their basic needs, let alone more complex thoughts and feelings. You are brave, you are amazing. I am humbled by the strength of your spirits. It is my hope that in some small way, I have shared my voice with you and adequately captured some of your challenges and victories.

I've made several writing buddies along the way, and I can count on one hand those who have become true partners. Anna H., Jackie C., and Krysti H., thank you for your willingness to read anything I ever sent you, sometimes for the hundredth time. Thank you for keeping the faith, for saying over and over again "and you *will* get published someday," and for being the reason for me to believe this assertion when I had no other reason to. You have a special place in my heart, right next to khakis and caribou and peppermint mochas.

Theresa H., Jen D., and Sally W., thank you for sharing your talents, opinions, time, and support. Thank you for never once making this feel like a competition, for always being so quick in responding, and for being awesome in general. Your friendship is swoonworthy and then some. Sandy H., Jenny E., Katie V., Temple W., and Kim K.—thank you all for being so uniquely cool and collectively supportive. I'm thrilled to be a part of this group.

CC, thank you for being my go-to girl every single day. Your support and friendship is invaluable.

Finally, thank you to my family: my nan, who always took pride in my artistic endeavors and told me I was "clever." Thank you to my parents and brother, who shared the attitude that everything I did was sort of amazing, naturally. This may not have always been the case, but their belief instilled a deep-rooted confidence (and stubbornness) in my ability to accomplish anything I wanted to achieve. Thank you to my Hamill/Feldman family members, for supporting me and this story in so many ways.

Thank you, James, for handling my aspirations with such care, respect, and seriousness. For every way you supported me, every step of the way. Thank you to my kiddos, for inspiring new levels of love on a daily basis and helping me understand and write the parent perspective in this story. With a little princess in a shimmering blue gown routinely belting out "have faith in your dreams and someday, your rainbow will come smiling through," how could I ever stop working toward mine? For all of this and more, my deepest appreciation—I love you all.

Turn the page for some

Sw♥♥nworthy

Extras...

A Coffee Date

with author Karole Cozzo and her editor, Holly West

"About the Author"

Holly West (HW): What was the very first romance novel you ever read?

Karole Cozzo (KC): I was thinking about this and what stands out in my head in terms of teen romance is the *Ocean City* series by Katherine Applegate. I just remember thinking they were so hot and scandalous when I was a teenager, particularly the second book, *Love Shack*. My friends and I were all reading them and they were the epitome of hot summer romance novels at that age.

HW: This is one of my favorite questions: If you were a superhero, what would your superpower be?

KC: I gave this one some thought and right now if I had a superpower it would be to expand time. So for every hour of normal time, I would be able to stretch it out so that it was about three hours of time in my world. So I could actually get all the things done that I want to get done in a given day.

HW: That is a *fabulous* superpower. If you were stranded on a desert island, who or what would you want for company?

KC: I was laughing about this with my husband, because when we were on our honeymoon, he actually opened a coconut for me using nothing but a seashell, and this was a really impressive feat he's never forgotten. So I guess if I were stranded on a desert island, somebody having that skill would be good to have around. Otherwise, I might just take my best friend because we both really need a vacation.

HW: How did you first learn about Swoon Reads?

KC: I got an email before the site started, probably because I was on the National Novel Writing Month website, and had done some work over there. I saw the initial email coming out a few months before the site actually went live, and I just kept checking around because I was really excited for it to get started and be up and running.

HW: I remember that you were one of the earliest members on the site. But not with *How to Say I Love You Out Loud*. Originally, you had uploaded something called the Broken trilogy. Why don't you talk a little bit about your original experience on the site?

KC: I really liked being one of the earlier people to be a part of the site launch because a community formed quickly among the earlier users. There are people from that original group that I still talk to everyday. So it's awesome in that way because I picked up a lot of writing companions. It felt very interactive at that point because it was a nice, small, contained group and everyone was talking with everyone and reading each other's stuff. That was a really good thing to be a part of.

And all along, there was a lot of thoughtful feedback. Once you get past the initial just-wanting-to-hear-that-people-like-your-story-and-like-your-writing, you really start to value the constructive criticism. There was actually a little bit of a thrill to it because it was like, "Ooh, a new tool. Something new to work with or a new angle to pursue." And people are pretty good about posting constructive criticism in addition to just the positive stuff. I've always had a really good experience on Swoon.

HW: What made you decide to take down *Broken* and post *How to Say I Love You Out Loud*?

Swoon Reads

KC: I really tried to be responsive to the information that I'd learned about the genre. I tend to want to write these long, sweeping, very slow, realistic progression stories. *Broken* itself was very long (three long novels) and I decided I really wanted to try playing by the rules. I wanted to take everything I'd heard about including too many details or having too slow of a buildup and really challenge myself and see if I could do it. So, from the beginning I outlined and set up *How to Say I Love You Out Loud* to work better as a standalone that was somewhere in the appropriate word range. For me, writing a shorter story was a huge accomplishment and I was really proud and excited to be able to share something totally different.

"About the Book"

HW: Where did you get the idea for this particular book?

KC: I've worked with students with disabilities for a long time and over the course of that, I've spent a lot of time working with their families as well. The sibling dynamic in those families has always interested me because many kids are forced to be mature from such a young age, and at times their needs are going to have to come second because there might be someone with more pressing or immediate needs. That's something that even adults struggle with, so I think for a child that can be especially difficult. I was also thinking about how we really do define ourselves in relation to our families—specifically, how their identity is defined by the fact that there's a person with a disability in their family. How does that make them feel during adolescence, a time of so much insecurity? How does that impact every relationship in their life? I just thought it would be interesting to explore. And I always liked writing about things in the context of romance, so I just took it in that direction.

HW: What was getting the edit letter like?

KC: The edit letter was kind of like an even better version of the constructive criticism from the site. Once you do the first read-over like, "OK, how bad is it going to be?" you realize, "OK, there's nothing that terrible. These people do like this book and do want to work with it." Pretty much every point I read through, when I took a minute to think about them individually, I felt like, "Yeah, I can see that, and I can see how that would make the book stronger." You want to make your first book as good as possible. After taking a few minutes to process, I was just really excited about it. It was a learning experience for me.

Typically, when I'm writing stories, my beginnings tend to be slow, and it's just sort of a personal preference for how I like things to unfold. But really thinking about what that means from a marketability perspective or the idea of getting people to pick up the book and want to read past the first chapter, then you start challenging yourself to do things in different ways and do things better. When you take it from that perspective, it's a learning process, and everything you do after that point can incorporate what you learned along the way. And, a lot of that came from the first edit letter. So it was pretty cool in the end.

HW: How does the revision process work for you?

KC: I definitely like to work with a hard copy. I like viewing the manuscript as a physical thing and, in terms of considering connectivity between chapters and constancy within characters, I like being able to flip back and forth through pages versus scrolling up and down on a computer. I like to have the entire manuscript in a binder in front of me. I went through after getting the edit letter and made notes on the pages or sections that needed to be worked on. And then I sort of divvied it up in terms of what was most important, what I needed to target first, and what was going to be the most time-consuming and started there. And then the minor details I worked on afterwards, with the thinking that if I was changing major things in another section, there was no point targeting the minor details until all of that was taken care of and I could go through and make sure everything lined up. I also knew I'd feel better fine-tuning small details and thinking more about individual wording once I got the bigger work or the harder work out of the way first. So I tackled it that way.

HW: I've found that that's a really logical way to do it. When I'm doing edits, I always ask, "OK, what is the biggest thing?" Then, "What are the medium things?" Then, "Are these things so big that all the little things that I have here should wait until the next draft?"

KC: My mind definitely works that way, too.

"The Writing Life"

HW: Where do you write? Do you have any writing rituals or do you write in a specific spot?

KC: No. I'm happy to write wherever I can set up my laptop. Surprisingly I do my most productive writing in busy places. If I can set up at a coffee shop, when there's some level of distraction, I actually can be the most focused on my story. While if I'm sitting in an empty, quiet room, I find it harder to concentrate. That's the only ritual I'd actually say I have. If there's a little bit of distraction going on, that's where I enjoy writing the most.

HW: What's your process? Are you a plotter and an outliner, or do you just make it up as you go along?

KC: I'm definitely an outliner to the nth degree. I really feel I need to know where characters are going, and knowing where they end up really impacts where they start. I've written stories where I haven't done that, and then I get to the end, realize what the character's motivation was, and it doesn't sync up with where they were at the beginning. That's really how I've decided to start outlining.

So, I'll start with my overall plot outline and really try to think through not only what's happening, but where the characters are at and probably will be. I'm more character based, so I tend to focus more on where the characters are at than the plot. Then I go through on a chapter-by-chapter basis when I'm writing and write a general outline of what's happening and bits of dialogue without punctuation or capitalization. Just sort of free-flow typing as it comes out. And then I'll go back that third time, start at the beginning of that chapter, and actually write it out. So it gets a little more specific each time I look at it.

HW: What is the very best writing advice you've ever heard?
KC: I can think of two pieces that I usually try to use to guide me. Number one is the old "Show, don't tell," and it's something you have to remind yourself all the time. Let the readers know what's happening through how the characters are talking and what they're doing in the moment rather than giving them the lengthy description of what's going on.

And the other really great piece of advice, I think, is "Write what you know." With *How to Say I Love You Out Loud*, it was a culture that I've just been immersed in for over a decade and I felt confident in what I was writing about and that I could do a realistic portrayal versus trying to talk about something that I had no experience with. I also think of Katie van Ark with *The Boy Next Door*. Katie was so clear in the writing that this was a culture that she was really a part of and it made the book a lot more realistic to me as a reader.

how to say *I Love You* out loud
Discussion Questions

1. Jordyn goes to great lengths to blend in at school and avoid attracting attention. Have you ever made sacrifices or choices you normally wouldn't in an effort to fit in? Why?

2. In Jordyn's place, would you keep your family a secret? Who would you tell, and why?

3. Have you ever had to give up on a crush to be "just friends" the way Jordyn originally did with Alex?

4. Did you empathize with Jordyn's reaction to Philip attending her school? Why or why not?

5. Do you think that Erin was right to be upset that Jordyn didn't talk to her about Philip?

6. Alex is building a playground for children with special needs. Have you ever participated in volunteer work like that?

7. Describe Jordyn and Philip's relationship. How does it change as the story progresses?

8. Which scene did you find the most romantic, and why?

9. Have you ever had to tell an important secret to someone you care about, like when Jordyn reveals the truth about her family to Alex? How did telling the secret affect your relationship?

10. Jordyn delivers an essay on the topic of "The Power of Speech." What does that mean to you?

Want to host your own
Swoon Reads Book Club Party?
Download our *free* event kit at
www.swoonreads.com/partykit!

Partners for life or just on the ice?

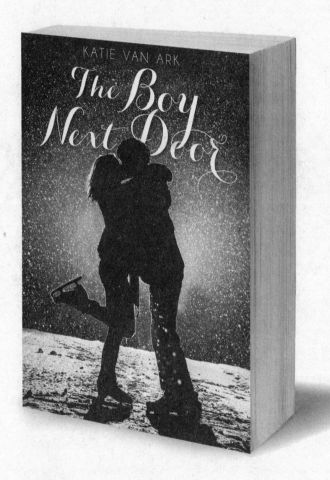

Will their new romantic skating program
be the big break Maddy's been waiting for,
or the big breakup that Gabe has always feared?

Gabe

A love story? This is some sort of deranged joke. Except Igor doesn't crack jokes. He barely knows how to smile.

I glance at Mad going all starry-eyed next to me. I've heard correctly. I look back at Igor and hold my eyes steady on him, but my insides are shaking worse than when I told Kurt I was quitting hockey just before the bantam travel team championships.

Igor nods his head toward our water bottles at the boards. "I leave copies of the music there. You listen at home tonight, yes? For today, we see what we have to begin." He cracks his knuckles under his leather gloves. "Death spiral again. Before, you skate for audience. This time? No audience. Only Madelyn and Gabriel. You understand?"

"Yes, sir." I understand, but there's an ice rink's chance in hell that I'm actually going to do what he wants. I take the lead and set my pivot, looking at the empty bleachers. It's been *Madelyn and Gabriel* for longer than I can remember. I let her hack off all my hair in preschool. I quit hockey for her. I broke my arm for her. There's nothing I wouldn't do for her . . . except this. She's like my sister, the way we read each other so well. Sib closeness, I can deal with. That's where it stops.

On the exit, I push out so my back is facing Igor and I stare over the top of Mad's head. Epic fail on my mission to fool our coach. "Again," he says. "You must look, Gabriel."

This time, I watch the skate on Mad's free foot as she circles around me. Igor is skating toward us before we've even finished the move. He nods at Mad. "Good, Madelyn. I have changed my mind. We listen to music now. Put it on."

Mad skates off, leaving me alone with the KGB. "I do not believe," Igor says. "*Make me believe.*"

I kick at the ice with my toe pick. Disrespectful, yeah, but a trip to the penalty box is sounding like a winning idea right now. I've known this day was coming. Known it since I first made myself look away from Mad's arched chest and . . . "I can't."

Igor steps closer, and I stop. I'm not sure what he'll do if I accidentally kick *him* but I'm sure I don't want to find out. His breath makes warm puffs of air in my face. "Do not tell me, 'I can't.' 'I can't' is not part of plan."

For years, I've trusted Igor's plans. For good reason. He's coached me and Mad to the national junior pair title and three Junior Grand Prix medals, including a fourth-place finish at the final last year. But . . . "This is Mad."

Igor's stainless steel eyes glint at me. "You want to win, yes?"

"Yes," I whisper. Mom's medals gleam in the back of my mind. I *need* to win.

"So you pretend. You need me to, what do we say, write it out?"

I don't need Igor to spell it out. I know how to get a girl going. Trouble is, I'm not so hot at *keeping* things going. Mad returns and I ease her into the move once again, this time to the long desperate notes of the music. I look at her face. "Sister, sister, sister," I chant to myself. But there's a cartoon red devil on my shoulder reminding me I'm an only child. Okay then: "Friend?"

My feeble attempt only spawns another devil. They slap each other five. "With benefits!" they chorus.

Where the hell are my angels? "No."

I must've said it out loud, because Mad startles. She slips off her edge and falls out of the spiral. She was only a few inches from the ice, but still. Stupidest move in the world to fall on. Even juvenile pairs do it in their sleep. I help her up. "Sorry."

"Madelyn," Igor says, his voice as sickly as a tornado-warning sky, "please go work on your brackets for a moment."

Igor's temper usually blows on Chris's shenanigans, but today, I get the twister cloud eyes. "I see you. All those girls, under bleachers at hockey games. What is problem here?" His gloved fingers curl, now black claws.

I look at Mad, zipping through her brackets. She attacks the twisty turns, the determination fierce on her face. She puts so much power into the pattern that she almost slams into the barrier at the end. That's the problem. I've compartmentalized my life for so long, but Mad has no fear of the barrier.

I look back at Igor, watching me watch Mad. His fingers have relaxed in his gloves. "Is pretend," he says, cajoling now. "But we are needing under the bleachers. Mind in storm drain."

If I let my mind go in the gutter, I'll never get it out.

"Madelyn," Igor calls. "Get a drink. We resume."

I skate over for a drink, too. Anything to stall.

Mad plunks her water bottle down on the barrier. She keeps her chin up but she doesn't look at me. "Am I that disgusting?"

"What?"

"You won't even look at me."

"No." Shiny dark brown hair. Eyes as wide and blue as summer sky. Cheeks splashed with such tiny freckles that I want to lean in close just to see them. Barrier. God, I need that barrier. "Mad. No."

"Forget it, forget I said anything." She skates back to Igor.

I follow, but this time, it's me stretching my hand out to her. Once more, we set up for the move. I do what Igor wants. I watch the white of Mad's neck as her head dips backward, let my eyes trail from those perfect collarbones over the bloomed arch of her chest. Mad's circling smoothly around me, but my whole world is waterfalling down the storm drain.

On the exit, my heart is pounding so loud I can't even hear the music. We present, arms locked out, free legs extended. But I can't stop. I take an extra stroke toward Mad, my face right up to those barely there freckles. "You're disgustingly beautiful." With my eyes locked on hers, I miss Igor's reaction. But I don't need even a nod to know this time was exactly what he wanted.

Looking for something else to make you swoon? Check out these other great Swoon Reads titles!

Fourteen viewpoints.
One love story.

Even her guardian angel
might have trouble
saving Cara . . .

First rule of dealing with
hot vampire bodyguards?
Don't fall in love!

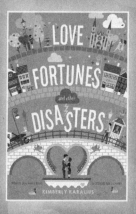

What if you were fated to
NEVER fall in love?

JCP Portraits

Karole Cozzo lives outside of Philadelphia with her loving husband, unendingly exuberant daughter, and eternally pleasant son. She is a school psychologist by day and a lover of all things colorful and creative by night. Karole spends her free time drawing with her young artists-in-residence, making photo books, decorating her home, and of course, writing. *How to Say I Love You Out Loud* is her debut novel. Find her online at kacozzo.com.